I0587655

TOO GOOD TO BE TRUE

Andrea Hunter

Too Good to be True

or How I met your father (UK-US edition)

First published in Great Britain in 2017 by Andrea Hunter via Type &
Tell

A CIP catalogue record for this book is available from the British Library

ISBN 978-1-78745-042-4

Typesetting via Type & Tell Book Editor

Type & Tell

To my beautiful and clever boys -
How wonderful life is, when you're in the world

About the Author

Andrea Hunter lives in Stockholm with her two teenage sons and her 7 year old substitute for a third child, her furry daughter Cookie: an energetic Ncva Scotia Duck Tolling retriever (also works as substitute for hairy man in bed). Working at a big television company in Sweden - THE major one in fact - as the head of production planning at the News department.

She started a blog in August 2015, at the one year anniversary of the first email, and the blog has now reached more than 15.000 views in 42 different countries. Mainly Sweden, Norway, Great Britain and the US, but also Australia, Asia and South America. When the book was published in Sweden she was invited to three morning shows on telly, got interviewed by three magazines and two of the biggest tabloids, both online and on paper. Being deceived and wanting reverge is a thing women - and men - can relate to. The feeling of getting lied to, getting dumped AND getting older.

But nobody puts Andrea in a corner. She is tired of being the sensible and understanding one - this is her revenge. And it will be served with a bittersweet love potion. Enjoy.

"You have always been a loving, caring and generous dad to us.
We love you."
J & A

PART 1.

THE STORY

ZERO

Tuesday August 12th, 2014

To: Andrea Hunter 2014-08-11, 09:32
From: Gemma Littleton
Subject: Dwayne

Hi Andrea,
I'm not sure if you know who I am - my name is Gemma and I am
Dwayne's girlfriend.

It is Tuesday at work, my second week after a four week vacation break. The summer outside the office is in its August peak and inside it's cool and work is a bit slow. At lunchtime I open my private email in my phone for a quick peek, and an email sent yesterday catches my eye.

Gemma Littleton? Who is that? The name Littleton rings a bell. Dwayne's girlfriend? What does she mean? My longtime long-distance boyfriend, as well as father of our children, my 'särbo' – Swedish term for lovers living apart (and in our case in different countries as well) – since 16 years.

Oh my God – something has happened to him! We haven't spoken for several days. Has he finally had a fatal heartattack? Is he in hospital and someone has been told to try to get hold of me? His hard working lifestyle has finally taken its toll. A name pops up in my head: Simpson Littleton – that's it – it is one of Dwayne's longtime friends! But Gemma?

I apologize for invading your privacy by contacting you like this but I need some answers and feel that you may be the only person that will be honest with me. Before I go into too much detail please reply to this and let me know if you are okay with it. I fully understand if you choose not to reply but I am hoping you will.
Once again sorry for the intrusion.
Hope to hear from you soon.
Regards,
Gemma

Gemma. Gemma. Dwayne's girlfriend? Girl friend. Friend that is a girl? I read the email again. And again. And then I text my best friend in the world, Sophie. Who is there for me in thick and thin.

Crisis. Call me.

It has now sunk in. She thinks she is Dwayne's girlfriend. I'M his girlfriend. What has he done to make her believe that SHE is?

In a blink of an eye my friend calls. I pop in to one of the small conference rooms to get some privacy.
"What's happened?" she asks with a voice that is prepared for every kind of response.
"I have got an email. From a Gemma."
I read the email to her.
"Oh, no. Dwayne. Fuck."

ONE

London calling

I remember when I first saw Dwayne.

I was in London with two of my friends in the summer of '98, after spending one crazy holiday week in Scotland.
Sophie. My best friend since high school. Like me blonde, green-eyed and tall, but with a slim figure unlike my more robust one.
Pamela. Tall as well, but with long, dark, silky hair and eyes the color of espresso.

All three of us were 31 and single. Young enough to have the energy, with firm bodies, wrinkle free skin and fresh looks, but old enough to be confident and know what we wanted, and grab it.

I had been single for almost 4 years, since my boyfriend at the time dumped me because he 'loved me – but not enough' to take it further with moving in together, and having children. I was heartbroken since it was my first REAL relationship with a normal man and I was infatuated by him. He was ash-blonde (very common in Sweden), normal height, normal built. I thought he was the sexiest thing on earth, after chasing Mr Tall Dark Stranger all my previous life. Let me tell you – Mr Tall Dark Stranger is also very, very illusive.

Sophie's boyfriend had decided to say thank you and goodbye a couple of years earlier, about the time when Sophie started thinking about babies (see a pattern here?). They were living together so she was pretty shocked when he handed in his notice.

Pamela had been in various relationships with foreign men, the last one a skinny french guy. She fancied everything that didn't speak Swedish, and she was now currently on the market.

The three of us were late bloomers Our mind and bodies developed late and whilst our classmates in the earlier teens were out discovering alcohol and the opposite sex, we were reading books (me), making home made clothes (Sophie) and playing football (Pamela). Sophie and Pammie had lost their virginities in their late teens, and I had reached the astonishing age of... T-W-E-N-T-Y-THREE when I got my cherry popped by a pilot. Unfortunately not on 10'000 meters - more like 10 meters up - if you count a flat on the 3rd floor. Sophie had been engaged and expecting a child in her early twenties, but sadly had an early miscarriage, and had moved on, both from family-making as well as her fiancé. We were now making up for lost time.

Pamela was the sensible one, and also a bit reserved. She always got the guys. Sophie and I had the guys swarming round us in a bar or a pub with our striking blonde looks and outgoing personalities. They were drawn to us like moths to a light, but while they laughed with us, and sang along or arm wrestled (somehow we always got them doing that), they eventually turned to Pammie who offered calmness and mystery all at once. She thought we were embarrassing but always thanked us politely after getting off with one of the good-lookers. Pammie was my second cousin actually, and we had known each other since we were newborn, but we could not be, and look, more different (except for both of us being tall).

We had printed up lime green T-shirts with the words Swedish B-cup tour on the chest, and the cities we were going to visit on the back, Edinburgh-London-Dublin. We wore them on the plane over to our first stop. We thought it was hilarious. The ambiguous message would give us the attention we wanted while on our trip (very immature - but as I said: we had some catching up to do as in being silly and reckless, usually a term reserved for the early twenty-something). We expected people (read: men) to ask us what it meant and we would have fun making them guess. We were all a cup B size-wise, at least Sophie and me. Pamela protested and considered herself being a C-cup but Sophie resolutely cupped her hands round her breasts and distinctively said 'Nope. Your B.' and that was that.

The first man who took notice of us in our screaming green T's was the air steward on the plane:

"So you all wear B-cups then?"

So much for being clever and making them guess.

"No, we're playing BASKETBALL actually. We're a team." I said and felt a bit silly. Not the reckless kind of silly, just - stupid.

We did recover from the setback and while in Scotland we did the following things, amongst others:

- sang out loud on an open top hop-on-hop-off tourbus throughout Edinburgh with Scottish hat/red wigs on (Sophie and I)

- knocked a guys front tooth out in a bar when he, un-welcomed, pinched Swedish girl-ass (I did. Didn't see that he had put the bottle to his lips. I just reacted instinctively to the pinch, and spun around while my palm flew out like a cobra and smacked him in the back of his head. Incredibly enough he didn't get angry, just grinned back at us with a toothless smile. Pretty hardened men those Scottish)

- threw up in a restaurant while trying haggis (Pamela)

- rolled around in fish guts after jumping down a brick

wall, straight into a bin, trying to get into the locked B&B via the backyard (Sophie)

- bought whisky-condoms and tried them out on our young tour-guide, who was driving the mini-van with a gang of us tourists round the Scottish highlands, after an extremely wet pub-night (if you continue reading you'll find out which one of us)

We were now on our way to Ireland for another week of partying, drinking and – some – sightseeing, but had decided to spend the weekend in London to meet up with English friends we knew from before and some Australian guys that Sophie and Pamela had met at an Elton John-concert in Gothenburg earlier that spring. We had been offered to stay in the Australian guys' house that they shared with some other people in Parsons Green.

We got a shock when we came to the Aussies' house. We had picked the key up from the civic center where they worked, these neat men in suits. Party animals sure – but with a neat touch. Nothing neat with the flat though. Mattresses were spread all over the floor, the bedlinen were everywhere but on the beds, and probably once white but not any more. And we found pubic hair on the phone! We were disgusted. Grown men in their thirties – how could they live like this? The kitchen was a mess as well. We found a furry thing in the oven that caught our interest. A cat? Or even a stuffed dog? But it turned out to be a - since long forgotten - loaf of bread that now was in full bloom in the oven. We looked at each other and simultaneously said: 'We can not stay here tonight!'. We got up, left the bags with the intention of picking them up later, and went to the nearest drinking place – an Aussie bar called the Southern Cross on Kings Road.

An hour later the neat but messy guys turned up. After having a go at them we continued, with them, to the corner pub on the opposite side of the small park – The White Horse. A busy place, buzzing with a great Friday-after-work-in-the-middle-of-July-feeling. People sitting, standing, drinking everywhere outside the pub.

Almost straight away when we got there I looked into a couple of hazelnut eyes placed in the face of a tall, dark-haired, broad-chested man standing behind a barrel placed just outside the pub. A beer in his hand and a big broad smile on his face, dressed like he just came from work – working with building or something similar. Irresistible. Our eyes locked for what felt like minutes. We continued drinking, me and my friends with the Aussies, and the hazelnut-eyed man chatted with a small funny-looking oldish man with grey hair. From time to time we checked each other out. I had a bubbly sensation in my stomach. Too much beer perhaps?

When it was time for us to leave and prepare us for continuing partying in the evening I walked ridiculously close to the man with the smiling face and his friend? workmate? and they said: 'Good evening girls', and I flashed back 'Good evening boys, or I mean: good afternoon men' (extremely silly even for me) and strutted off in my flowery, grey summer-dress.

And that was that. I thought.

* * * * * * * * * * * * * * * * * * * *

Tuesday August 12th, 2014.
Afternoon.

When I come out of the little conference room, I feel like there is no floor under my feet. I hear the little helper in my head speak with a soothing voice. I don't know if the voice is female or male, but I hear 'Okay, let us switch on to autopilot now. Legs - check, arms - check, vision - check. We are fine. Just relax and enjoy the ride'.
Suddenly a person is standing in front of me. It is one of my co-workers and I can see her lips moving.
'Vision!! What the fuck are you doing?!'
'Sorry!! I didn't see her coming! I was focusing on the desk!'
'Alert! Alert! We need to get her to act completely normal! All systems alert! Need as many as possible to the lips. Call in a.s.a.p!' my little helper roars in my head. 'AND GET SOME BLOOD TO THE CHEEKS!!'
"What?"
I feel confused. It is absolutely chaos in my head.

"Eh, can I have five minutes? I need to discuss something with you."

When Erin asks for five minutes it is more likely to be fifty. I can't think of any excuse to not say okay to five (or even fifty) minutes. It is absolutely dead calm at work. None to pretend that I must see for a meetirg.

'Toes? Can you get up to the lips now? We don't need you down there.'

'But it is so far. Do we really have to? What if we need to curl them up all of a sudden?'

'OK, I hear you! Ears - you are closer. Get your ass over to the lips. NOW!'

'Hey! I can't work under conditions like this!'. My brain raises its voice. 'If I can't hear what's coming in, I don't know what to put out. SISO you know, Shit In - Shit Out.'

Grumpy old sod.

'Okay, okay, I hear you. Nose - we definitely don't need you right now, get to the lips!'

"Of course, Erin."

'We're already there!' something squeaks in my head.

"Let's go and sit somewhere and talk."

'TOES! Action! Get up to the knees, they're wobbling - we need more support! And get those feet MOVING! We need to get her down on a chair before she falls!'

I chose another room for this talk. Erin lays out a dilemma to me. I answer mechanically, using words that I know I've used before in similar situations, but am not sure that I now put them together in the right context. But Erin seems pleased, and content that I have given her some tools to solve the dilemma. Probably a hammer to use on a screw, but hopefully she will discover that later. After 35 minutes I excuse myself and say that I just remembered that I need to send an email before everyone leaves for the day, and then I stare at the computer for two hours before I make my way home. I feel dizzy.

I call Dwayne in the afternoon. No answer. I try again. The phone is ringing but the answering machine starts. I send him a text.

Got an email from Gemma Littleton. Sounds like you haven't just been working... She wants me to contact her – shall u and I speak first?

I feel that my heart is steady as a rock. My mind is crystal clear, no blurry emotions to get me unfocused. This needs to be sorted out. Is this Gemma a madwoman? And what if he says she is – can I trust him?

4 hours later I still haven't got a response. I text him again, feeling no hope he will answer.

If you have texted me I haven't got it. Hopefully you're mature enough by now to give me a call back even if it's a bit unpleasant.

The answer comes an hour later.

At the football call u tomorrow x

Is he mad? Has he totally lost his marbles? At the football? It's a fucking crisis here and he can't call me because HE IS AT THE FOOTBALL?! It's odd, but somehow the text has a calming effect on me after a while. He doesn't think this is a big deal. She certainly must be a mad woman that is hanging after him. So what if they've had a shag, it happens even in the best of relationships that a partner jumps over the relationship-fence under the influence of alcohol, or something else. It hasn't happened to me though - I've been able to stay on the right side of our fence. But you know, many others….

I have to talk to him before I answer Gemma. It is important. I read Gemma's email again and after the last line I discover another sentence when scrolling down on the phone.

Please don't let Dwayne know I've contacted you - he would not be happy about it.

Oh well. Too late for that now girl. He is MY boyfriend and he is the one I turn to. Crazy bitch.

Wednesday August 13th, 2014

In the morning light, as I wake up after a terrible night's sleep with tossing and turning, I see things differently. What if? What if she is not insane and I talk to Dwayne and he denies it all? And if she IS his girlfriend maybe he convinces her to not have any contact with me and I'll be outside any kind of information. Is it better to make contact with Gemma now to get things rolling? After all – I have given him a chance to contact me but he chose THE FOOTBALL! Bloody Englishmen with their football mania. I look at our beautiful boys deeply asleep, totally unaware of the turmoil in their mother's stomach and head.

To: Gemma Littleton 2014-08-13, 09:17
From: Andrea Hunter
Subject: Re: Dwayne

Hi Gemma.
I didn't see your email until yesterday.
I didn't know about you and got in a bit of a shock and I didn't see the last bit (it was outside the phone-frame) so I have contacted Dwayne.
If you have questions I will try to answer them as honestly as I can (but remember that it will be my point of view - Dwayne, if I know him right, will probably have another story).
First answer a couple of mine:
- Are you a sister of Dwayne's friend Simpson Littleton?
- When did you and Dwayne start dating?

- How long have you considered yourself to be his girlfriend?
- How did you get this email-address?
It will be interesting to hear from you.
Andrea

There. Let's see where this takes us.

I can't focus at work. My mind is spinning. I talk to Sophie at least five times during the day. Is it a new relationship? How long has it been going on for? Since this spring? Or even for one or two years? I can suddenly relate to Gemma knowing what I know about Dwayne. So secretive. Not letting anyone too close. Not communicating, and as soon as something gets a bit rocky he chooses to just disappear for a couple of days. If they are dating she probably wants to try to take him into a new phase of their relationship. And if they are a couple of years down the line she probably wants to go the distance and take it even further. Like getting engaged. Or moving in together. Christ. The more I think about it, our physical relationship had started to cool off a couple of years ago. But I'm no expert – isn't that to be expected after so many years together? Even if in a long-distance relationship? I suddenly get a vague unpleasant feeling. What if? What f it has been going on even longer?
I bury that feeling deep down. That is not possible. Dwayne is working too much. Too much. And with his heart-condition he couldn't cope with that. Nope.

At lunchtime a girl that I used to work with, in the early days at work, calls. I had totally forgotten that we had booked a lunch date and I'm on the verge of canceling it but then I think that I need to focus on something else, to give my brain a break to not melt down to porridge. I can't tell Ella about this though. I feel ashamed. That I should have known better than to think that it works to have a long-distance relationship with a man. I am not ready to burst the, what now starts to look like a bubble, image of my life as a 'strong-successful-independent-woman-and-mother-of-two-with-a-loving-man-close-in-heart-and-mind-but-physically-on-a-distance'.

"I have just received an email" is the first thing that slips out of my mouth when we sit down after the usual greeting hugs outside the sushi-place just around the corner from work.

When we hug, her brown, soft waist-length hair gets entangled in my arms and I get flashbacks of my life and who I was before I met Dwayne and I feel the urge to talk about it. And I realize as soon as I see her that I can't act normally. I feel like I am seeing myself from above. I feel very grown up and sensible as I lay out the hard facts:

- what I know (very little)

- what I don't know but what I think has happened. 'Going on for a couple of years, understandable, it has cooled off between us for the last couple of years, not much to do about it' etc etc etc.

"Aren't you angry?" she asks as she looks with her brown questioning eyes straight into mine.

"These things happen" I answer. "One has to be grateful that the kids are a bit older now. I just want to know what happened and try to understand it, and maybe learn something from it. The difficult thing right now is to not have the facts. Hell, it could have been going on for ages!" I say and laugh. "No, it is more likely that it has been one, or maybe two, years. It seems long but since we've been on a distance it could have been possible."

My lunch with Ella sets my memory jogging. He did start to diet a little more than a year ago. Lost several pounds. After he turned 50. Ah – a mid life crisis – that's it! Very common. Sophie's husband just got up from their couch before he turned 50 – after losing loads of weight and for the first time had a fit figure – and said that he didn't like it in their house and he wanted to move. She said okay – where shall we move then? He just said, matter of factly, that he wanted to move out himself. Without her. That was almost two years ago and she has just started to get back on her feet. What is it with men? Of course, it must have been going on at least a year between Gemma and Dwayne. Okay, I'm fine with that. We could either sort it out or just break up. Nothing that hasn't happened to others.

Oh, no. Turning 50. When he asked 'permission' to go to Las Vegas on a trip that his rich business partner treated him with. Dwayne was so happy that I didn't nag on him about it. 'You are so special!' Why would I nag? It was a fantastic gift. And it saved me from getting him a special present. I could never top that. I was quite pleased actually, it took the pressure of me. It feels a bit different now that it is a pretty good chance that he didn't go to Vegas with his boss. But with Gemma. His girlfriend. His OTHER girlfriend.

He said he would call me. I text him.

Don't forget to call me. Now is a good time.

Silence.

TWO

Destiny is calling - 'Come home with me'

Quite late that first evening in London we came to a Spanish bar called La Rueda (closed down now. What a coincidence). Everyone in high spirit. We had met up with one of our English friends – this one named Pete. A proper neat man that I met a few years before while taking Spanish lessons in Madrid. We had convinced him to lend us the key to his Islington flat so we didn't have to stay in the pubic-hair-on-phone den – didn't matter how charming the Aussie guys living in it were – and we were dancing, drinking, laughing and having a really good time. Suddenly someone grabbed my arm on the dance-floor. It was that funny-looking small guy from earlier at The White Horse.

"Hi!" I yelled, trying to get heard in the pumping music. "Where is your good looking friend?!"

He turned around and pointed in the corner where I could see hazelnut-eyes trying to balance against the wall, smiling at me.

"Ahhha!" I shouted and danced to him, grabbed him by the arm and pulled him out on the dance-floor.

"I don't really dance" he said.

"Well you're gonna dance with me!" I answered and he did.

Of all the places in London – what is the odds of ending up in the same place? It must be destiny! I held on to that for many years, and kept coming back to that feeling for the future decisions I made. We had met for a reason! The father of my children! It wasn't until years later I realized that La Rueda wasn't that far away from The White Horse, and if you were living in the area it wasn't strange at all that you started at a pub in Parsons Green and ended up at La Rueda on Kings Road. I didn't grip the London surroundings back then (and I was a bit drunk during the whole trip).

The tall dark stranger and I got all sweaty on the dance-floor, and after a while we had to get out to get some fresh air. We almost instantly started kissing. The attraction was immediate and strong, and fueled by beer and Margaritas. He pressed my back against an iron fence and we had our hands all over each other.

"Come home with me" he mumbled into my ear.

I was crazily excited but not totally out of control – I knew we had to get our luggage from that horrible house and I couldn't just lose track of my friends.

"I'd love to but I can't" I answered and got out of his grip. "But you can help us save our bags from a horrible bachelors nest! I'll see you at The White Horse tomorrow."

* * * * * * * * * * * * * * * * * *

Thursday August 14th, 2014

When I wake up after another restless night I have a new email from Gemma.

To: Andrea Hunter 2014-08-13, 23:19
From: Gemma Littleton
Subject: Re: Re: Dwayne

Hi Andrea,
Thanks for getting back to me. In answer to your questions:
Yes I am Simpson's sister.
Dwayne and I started dating in February 2002.

Wait a minute. Wait. A. Minute. Two thousand and TWO? I read the year over and over. 2002. It must be 2012? Surely? Our youngest son is BORN 2002. In April.

*We split up for approximately 3 weeks in January 2007 when he
came to see you in Sweden (that was not the reason we split up).
He told me he stayed in a boarding house near to where you live
but knowing what I do now I don't think that's true!!*

Oh. My. God. The extent of his deceiving is sinking in to my
heart like a razor sharp knife.

*When I met Dwayne he told me he had a young son in Sweden but
he did not have very much contact.
I accepted this as his past was nothing to do with me. He never
mentioned you or your son - the only thing I ever saw was a photo
of your son at his Mum and Dad's house.*

Son? What is she on about? Sons. It is sonS.

*When he came back from Sweden I asked him why he was so
secretive about the situation and I said it would be nice if we went
to Sweden for a few days and I could meet his son. He agreed and
said we would. Months passed by and there was still no mention
of any contact. Every time I asked if you had been in touch he
would become evasive and I began to think he was lying.*

*We carried on with our lives together - he lives with me and stays
at Ellen and Paul's once a week.*

Ellen and Paul. Dwayne's parents. So – they are all in on it.
Oh the feeling of betrayal.

I do the administration work for Dwayne's building company and in January this year as I was going through the emails I saw that one had been sent to you (that's how I got your email address). It was photos of Dwayne, Sebastian, Paul and your son. I got such a shock as I knew nothing about this visit. Dwayne said you had been over once to London.

Once? What IS this? My heart starts racing.

A week after seeing the photos we went on holiday to Egypt. On the last day of the holiday we were talking about life in general and I asked him if he thought he may have any other children that he might not know about. I could tell from his reaction that he was hiding something. He said he did not want to talk about it - I would not let it go and kept pressing him. Imagine my shock when he told me he did have another son with you. He said he could not remember how old he was. He said he did not see him until he was 16 months old.

I almost start to heave. He has denied the existence of his youngest son for... 12 years. His whole life. In a big part of Dwayne's life he has pretended that our beautiful gorgeous Alexander doesn't exist. The boy he talks so much football with. Our son who is a devoted Chelsea fan just like him. Who adores his dad. Suddenly the fact that there is another woman isn't a big deal at all. THIS is. A MAJOR BIG DEAL. I feel nauseous. And a rage is starting to build up. As well as a flood of tears.

I knew he was lying about so much so I found you on Facebook (you were a friend of Catherine, Dwayne's sister-in-law).
I saw from the photos that there was a lot of contact. Even though there were no photos of Dwayne I guessed that you were together in the Isle of Wight. When I questioned him about this he told me you arrived at Ellen and Paul's house one day without warning and asked him to go to the Isle of Wight with you.

I am getting really angry. He makes ME sound like a madwoman. I no longer think that Gemma is. Although I never imagined that he could do something like this, I now have no doubt that her story is true. It sounds just like him. What an incredibly utterly lying coward.

My questions to you are very personal but I need the truth.
Did you get pregnant after I started dating Dwayne?
Have you stayed in a hotel with him when you have visited London?
Did you share a room in the Isle of Wight?
Have there been any other holidays?
Do you email/text/ring him on a regular basis?
Andrea, you are right about Dwayne - he will have a different story but I cannot believe a word he says.
Look forward to hearing from you.
Gemma

Look forward to hear from me? Poor girl. She has no idea. I text Dwayne.

**What a first class prick you are. I don't want you to
disappear from the boys. Just call them whenever you
want. I won't tell them about this for a while. I know
everything. If you would have called me yesterday I could
have spared Gemma the details but not now when you're
acting like such a coward by not calling. Andrea**

Best to put my name in the text if there are more women
out there. I don't understand how I can act so coolly. Then I
email Gemma.

To: Gemma Littleton 2014-08-14, 08:01
From: Andrea Hunter
Subject: Re: Re: Re: Dwayne

*Hi again. Forgive me, I have to melt this since it's worse than I
thought. Here is info about our sons:*
*Jason, born -99, and Alexander, born April 2002. Dwayne came
to us when Alexander was 6 weeks (according to him he was in
jail after a fight when he was born and waiting for court - that's
why it took so long). According to them their mum and dad are
together - loving each other but living apart. I thought so too,
even if our physical intimacy faded out a couple of years ago. I
thought that was due to his heart-medicines.*
*I'll try to answer all your questions later today when I have cooled
off and can think straight.*
Andrea

What a fool I have been.

THREE

What a man!

The Saturday came and just after noon my friends and I headed towards The White Horse again. I started to get a little bit nervous. Was hazelnut-eyes going to be there? How should I act? Should I try to be cool and pretend not to see him and then nod to him a bit coolly. Or was it better to just walk up to him, give him a hug and a peck on the cheek and then take it from there? Was he in to me at all or was it just a drunken thing that happened last night?

It was packed outside the pub, the sun was out and again it was a warm and beautiful day. As we closed in on the crowd I suddenly saw his back. Big, strong and beautiful. My heart leaped when he turned around – he looked like a mixture between a young Marlon Brando with lips like my favorite actor Paul Newman – and when he saw me a big

Gene Kelly smile broke up in his face. He grabbed me by the waist, pulled me against him, asked me if I wanted a beer and then led me into the pub. In there he put his hands round my head and gave me a lovely long promising kiss. Wow! My kind of man! Big, strong, handsome AND taking initiative!

* * * * * * * * * * * * * * * * * * * *

To: Gemma Littleton 2014-08-14; 13:55
From: Andrea Hunter
Subject: Re: Re: Re: Re: Dwayne

Gemma - this is a nightmare. I don't know if I should laugh or cry. Still in shock probably.
Sebastian wasn't in the photos you saw: it was of our sons, Jason (15) and Alexander (12), from our trip to London this January.

Answers to your questions:
1. Did you get pregnant after I started dating Dwayne?
No, but it feels terrible that I was 7 months pregnant with our second child and still under the impression that we might move together sometime - and he was out dating.
2. Have you stayed in a hotel with him when you have visited London?
We have stayed at Ellen & Paul's. Me & Dwayne in his bed in his room on the top floor, or one of the boys in his bed and I in one of the other bedrooms with our other son as they grew older. Since the fall 2002(?) we have been over to London 2-4 times a year

35

(depending on how many times Dwayne have been over to Stockholm), 3-6 nights every time.

3. Did you share a room in the Isle of Wight?

Yes - room and bed. Every trip to IoW.

4. Have there been any other holidays?

Yes. Three trips to Isle of Wight:

Last summer (-13) together with Dwayne, the boys, Ellen & Paul.

Two summers before that with only me, Dwayne & the boys.

And one trip there with Dwayne, Sebastian & the boys in the fall a year before (-10).

We also have been at EuroDisney and Paris one fall (2009): me, Dwayne, Sebastian & the boys.

Ellen & Paul has got a photo-book of all the trips (except from last summer). That includes a photo from Dwayne & Sebastian's trip to Stockholm in Aug/Sept 2012. Dwayne & I shared my bed then.

5. Do you email/text/ring him on a regular basis?

Yes. The first years, and when both kids were small, several times a day. Then a couple of years with at least once a day, and now as the boys English is fluent we speak or text a couple of times a week (sometimes less) and Dwayne calls the boys directly.

More info (if you want it):

Dwayne has been here several times, mostly for long weekends. 1-2 times a year when the kids were younger, but after his heart failure 2003? 2004? (if that really happened of course...) it's been more seldom. He's stayed in my house, in my bed.

I've never 'just showed up' in London. I've told him well in advance when I'm planning to come over with the boys, and he has participated in the planning of our holiday trips. Sometimes I have booked them and sometimes he has booked them.

June 2007 (when I turned 40) he was here for almost a month. He went back to London and came back a few weeks later with the intention of moving here. He got cold feet after a week and went back again. Then he returned in January 2008, again with the intention of moving here, but went back to London after 3 weeks. As I recall it he rented a flat in London round 2007/2008. We stayed in it once when we were over during that period.

I have to pause my writing for a bit. Gemma wrote that they split up in January 2007. It must have been 2008. How can she be so sure that they didn't split up because of me? Where in all this came Dwayne's decision to move to Sweden, first in 2007 and then 2008? Was it when they had broken up? Or did he actually take the step and tried to finish it off with her to have a go for a life with me and his boys? Was I the second choice when the relationship with Gemma didn't work, or was I his first? I have trouble picturing Dwayne actually make a conscious choice so probably the first alternative. I feel a pang of sadness. And I start doubting myself. Have I only imagined that we were in a proper relationship? Have I fooled myself and everyone around me?

I'm sorry if the dates and years are wrong. As I said: still in shock. Our sex-life has been on hold since I turned 40, I can count the times we had sex on the fingers of one hand (sorry for being direct). I've thought his impotence was due to his heart-medicine. Probably caused by severe guilt I realize now. We've always been

37

cuddly and kissing in bed though. Been less of that the last couple of years.

Late in June this year he had a disproportionally big outburst about Facebook and me publishing a picture of him - I now understand why.
I'm sorry for this. I've been so focused on my own shock and pain but I realize that this can't be easy for you either.

This bitch has destroyed my relationship with Dwayne but I feel some sympathy for her and some kind of sisterly connection (if that exist – or maybe I'm just going mad) and of course I realize that this is all Dwayne's doing and that she is as fooled as I am.

I hope you have someone you can talk to about this. Since my & Dwayne's relationship slowly has faded you don't have to worry about any competition from me if you want to try to repair your relationship with him. But I don't want him to disappear from the boys lives and I will do my best to keep this civilized so the boys don't get hurt.

I have often thought that a strong relationship survives an infidelity. But this is not just infidelity. This is major betrayal. And the feelings I had left for him, like a constant burning glow under the ashes, had efficiently been wiped out after reading Gemma's last email. Like someone had splashed a giant bucket of water on it.

I do have more questions if you can answer them:
- Do you and Dwayne have kids together? (Need to know)

A girlfriend on the side. A child with her is the thing that could make it even worse.

- When did he move in with you? (Want to know to try to understand and lay the puzzle)

Since I know that I will never get any answers from Dwayne I hope you and I can maintain contact. I know the phases of shock and more questions will rise as time passes.
I will probably have to go to London with the boys when things have calmed down a bit, to establish some form of communication with him so that the boys don't lose contact with him or their grandparents. Maybe in the fall (or even further on - I don't know how long this will take). You and I might even meet up for a drink - anything that will be needed to get closure on this. At least it would piss Dwayne off....

Now I realize that we're past the point of rescue (to quote one of my favorite country&western songs with Hal Ketchum). I email Dwayne's parents. Might as well go the distance.

To: Ellen Peterson 2014-08-14, 15:12
From: Andrea Hunter
Subject: I know everything about Gemma Littleton and Dwayne's charade

FOUR

"See you later"

That Saturday at The White Horse, several hours were spent snogging with hazelnut-eyes – that I by then knew was named Dwayne – and drinking beer and chatting away with him and his friends. Except for that small funny-looking grey-haired guy who's name was Tom, a strikingly good-looking man in working pants covered in paint also had joined us. Tall, brown wild hair and a beautiful face. Simpson Littleton. I only had eyes for Dwayne though and I really enjoyed his tight grip around my waist. It was such a perfect afternoon. We all decided to meet up later that evening. The Aussies were still with us and had mentioned a place where we would probably end up, and I got Dwayne's phone number to give him a ring when we were on our way. Tom took my number just in case (which was a bit odd since it was Dwayne and I who quite obviously were glued together) and then we split up with a 'see you tonight'.

* * * * * * * * * * * * * * * * * * *

To: Andrea Hunter 2014-08-15, 01:50
From: Gemma Littleton
Subject: Re: Re: Re: Re: Re: Dwayne

Andrea - you are right, this is a nightmare. I have decided to cry!!!

I cannot believe what I have just read. Thanks for your honesty.
I will email you tomorrow as I need time to take this all in.
I have just opened a bottle of wine to see me through probably one of the worst nights of my life.
I'm so sorry for the both of us.

Will be in contact tomorrow.

Gemma

* * * * * * * * * * * * * * * * * * *

Ring, ring – if only you'd give me a call

When I called Dwayne in the evening to let him know where we were, just a few hours after leaving his embrace at the pub, I got straight to voicemail. I got the right hump. So – he wasn't more eager than this? I did not swallow my pride at all, or even gave it a second thought why the answering machine had started – I just turned my own phone off. There you go – you've had your chance mister! I was very miserable though. Pamela had fallen big time for one of the Aussies, Mick - who actually was from New Zealand, and Sophie was in the arms of Aussie-Jed, so I was feeling very left out. I ended the evening early and went to the Islington-flat on my own.

When Sunday came none of my friends had come back. Round noon they called. By their ecstatic voices I could tell that they had started drinking again, and they asked me to join them in Hammersmith. I was pissed off with my friends for not coming back that night, irritated that I had been stood-up by Dwayne, and indulged in self pity, so I sulkily said no and intended to stay in the flat forever on my own. Or at least until it was time for us to continue our trip, and head for Ireland on the Monday.

I was thinking of Dwayne and his strong arms and smiling face. I felt so extremely lonely. Should I – could I – give him a call? My pride got in the way, I didn't seem that important to him, and the fact that I had to scrub up and show myself from my best side if I did meet up with him felt impossible at the time. And I definitely didn't want to get the voicemail again so I let go of that idea.

Instead I found a cd of Bob Dylan, who I never listen to normally, and played the song 'Hurricane' over and over. I was totally mesmerized by the lyrics and Dylan's voice. Getting 'falsely tried', put in prison for 'somethin' that he never done'. By what must have been the fiftieth time I was cured! Sun was shining, I was in London, and my best friends were in Hammersmith – of course I would go to them! And Dwayne was all forgotten...

* * * * * * * * * * * * * * * * * * * *

To: Andrea Hunter 2014-08-15, 21:21
From: Gemma Littleton
Subject: Re: Re: Re: Re: Re: Re: Dwayne

Hi Andrea,
With a heavy heart and an aching head I type this email.
The wine I drank last night did not help me sleep.
I had to re-read your email several times before the facts sunk in and I've spent all night going over and over its content.

Let me tell you what has happened.
After reading your email I confronted Dwayne late last night and in true Dwayne style he began to deny everything - he ran

upstairs and started packing a bag. He was like a rabbit caught in the headlights. He left the house and drove off.

I can't help myself and start laughing. I have no trouble at all picturing Dwayne. I lose every bit of respect that I might have had for this man. What a coward. And I enjoy imagining how stressed and panicked he must have felt. Serves him right.

I called him on his mobile and we talked for a long time. He admitted everything you said apart from being unfaithful - he said he had not slept with you since Alexander was born (he knows how strongly I feel about being faithful).

How can he even think that it is not worth to tell the truth, the whole truth and nothing but the truth? Does he think we are stupid?

Andrea, I would love to say I believe Dwayne but I know in my heart that you are telling me the truth (at least I hope you are).

Eh...? How can she even doubt that?

Okay, a little background information:
Dwayne got married to his second wife in 1998 (I think it was April though I cannot be sure of the month). I'm sorry if this is another shock for you as I'm sure Dwayne would not have told you he was married when you got together.

My God. It could get worse. I met Dwayne in 1998. In July. He had been married 3 months. Give or take one month or two... No wonder he didn't answer his phone when I called him that evening. He was married!?!! But he asked me to come home with him?

I start to think about when Dwayne and I first made love a month after meeting each other that first weekend in London. Or had sex. I'm getting a bit confused now what it was we had. In the warm post coital glow (oh how I love that fantasy word – in reality we probably were sweaty, tired and a bit hungover...) he told me about his son, Sebastian, 9 years old. I sat up in bed and I remember I asked him straight out: 'Are you married?'. 'Divorced' he answered. Well that was correct. Only he was married also. With his second wife. How could I have been so stupid?

Kate was his first wife (they got married when Dwayne was about 25) - Sebastian's Mother.

As I already told you I met Dwayne in Feb 2002 at which point he was still married.

He was married when we made Alexander. While we were together in Sydney, Australia. Mad y in love.

I was living with my partner and had a daughter who was 8 years old at the time. Within a week of meeting each other we had left our partners. Dwayne moved out of his marital home and back in with his parents. I moved out of the home I shared with my partner and moved into the house I live in now.

Talk about betting on the wrong horse.

Can you believe that at one point in his life Dwayne had a wife, a pregnant girlfriend and a new girlfriend all at the same time?

I suddenly start to feel like I'm in a movie. Doesn't feel as bad. It is a thrilling story. What is going to happen next?

If I remember correctly Dwayne was in Spain with me when he told you he was in prison. He denies he said this and says he did not see his son when he was 6 weeks old - again who do you think I believe!!
Of course you must have seen the tattoo on his arm - that's my name in Chinese writing. He had that done a couple of months after we got together. I would be interested to hear how he explained that.
In answer to your questions:
Kids together:
No, we do not have children together - I only have my daughter who is 21

I feel a bit comforted with this information. At least I'm special. I'm the only one he has got two kids with.
...Or am I? Maybe he has got even more children? That even Gemma don't know about?

When he moved in:
Dwayne has been staying here most nights for about 5 years - no wonder he always had to keep a room at his Mum and Dad's - I

suppose he told you he lived there.

I am still trying to understand how his Mum and Dad have been able to face the both of us.

Dwayne and I went to the Isle of Wight in October 2012 with Ellen and Paul to celebrate their 40th wedding anniversary. How could they have done that knowing their son was cheating on 2 women?

I am still so raw I cannot even get my thoughts in order.

I have close friends who I can talk to but what's the point, they have no idea what this feels like.

I have one friend who would chop Dwayne's balls off if I told her the full story!!

Why isn't she telling them the full story? Chopped off balls would be a good start to get even.

Andrea, this has been so painful for us both but in a strange way it has been a comfort to know that I am not alone - we have both been taken for fools!!

Who knows what's going to happen now. We must keep in contact and we will meet up for a drink or two when you come over. I have an idea: You, me and Dwayne go for a drink in Putney - we get him drunk and throw him off Putney bridge, at least that way he would no longer be a menace to women!!!

Get back to me with your thoughts.

Gemma

To: Gemma Littleton 2014-08-16, 00:26
From: Andrea Hunter
Subject: Re: Re: Re: Re: Re: Re: Re: Dwayne

My thoughts? Let's meet up for a drink with Dwayne, Ellen AND Paul and throw them ALL in the river.

This is just crazy - I've gone hysterical after reading your email. I can't stop laughing. The image of rabbit-Dwayne is so spot on, and the info about Dwayne being married a second time and being married DURING our first years is just too much. Thank you for confronting him - I hope he suffers deeply. I don't think I'll ever get the chance since he probably will avoid me.

Of course we have had sex after Alexander was born. How can he even think that it's worth to continue the lying?? Or is he living so strong in denial that his memory has gone blank? But as I said: our sex-life has faded over the years. But the cuddles, kisses and "I love you's" have always been there.

I sent an email to Ellen yesterday and told her that I know about Dwayne's charade (I understood by your email that they must be aware of Dwayne's double-life). I don't want them to lose contact with the boys and I wanted them to know that the blame is Dwayne's. Imagine my surprise today when I got Ellen's reply: she was so sorry I found out about this. "We live after the old saying - what you don't know won't hurt you." Not a word about that they think their son has done something wrong. They were more interested in knowing who told me, which I didn't tell them. I now think that they all must be psychopaths in that family. How the hell can they think that this is okay as long as no one knows???? And every time when we've been over - all the pictures of the boys in the living room, and of me and the boys in Dwayne's room - have they all been a part of 'setting the scene' for our arrival???

Since I love to take photos I have loads of proofs of Dwayne's visits here and of us in London. If you're ever in doubt. Beautiful pictures of a 6-week-old Alexander in the sunshine in his fathers strong tattooed arms... Very painful to think about that now. The tattoo? "It's all my boys names in Chinese" I was very happy about it. Now I wish I knew Chinese at that time....

I think he's blamed prison a couple of times. One New Year when I was pregnant and hysterical and couldn't reach him to say 'Happy New Years'. When it comes to Alexander's birth it might have been that he blamed he was waiting for a court date. I might be mixing up his excuses for not showing up, or for not being able to stay here with us. They have been so many: prison, court-dates, not finding passport, missing flights, loads of work, burglary in the flat, Sebastian needs to be sorted out, fear of flying etc etc...

Feels like you are my only lifeline to answers - THANK YOU for being brave enough to contact me! I still haven't spoken to Dwayne. Feels like I have nothing to say and that there is nothing I want to hear from him. Must get in contact some day though and let him know that I won't stand in the way for his relationship with the boys. They love, adore and need him.
Keep in touch!!
Andrea (Margaritas is my painkiller for the night).

For some reason I feel comforted by the emails from Gemma. It is weird. I actually like her. And it feels good that she is actually even more fooled by Dwayne than I am. I didn't ask him questions, well aware that he could so easily chose to lie, since I couldn't check from a distance. She has asked the questions and he has lied to her. Big time.

FIVE

What A MAN!!

On the Monday morning we flew off to Ireland. A rented car took us around the green island. Small villages, monasteries, whiskey distilleries and cute B&B's. It was lovely, but we had also started to get on each others nerves. After drinking constantly throughout Scotland and London we were now forced to keep sober during the days due to driving, and lack of sleep had taken its toll. And I was still a bit irritated that Sophie and Pammie hadn't come home that Saturday night in London. I was the only one with a mobile phone (imagine!) and what if we had lost track of each other? (I had a slight bigger touch of control-mania back in those days and I didn't like to not know what's going to happen next. Boy – have I learned to get patient over the years...).

After five days of driving around the countryside, with regular outburst of nagging, we entered Dublin. The final stop. The last weekend of our 18 day trip. We checked in at Harcourt Hotel on Harcourt Street – that we on more than one occasion mispronounced as 'Hardcore' to everyones joy – and then went out to start our last drinking-spree in the Temple Bar. We had heard so much about it but didn't think much of it. It was just packed with too many drunk people, and the smell of sweat and spilled beer. And we didn't think we got the attention we deserved. After entertaining (in our opinion – if you asked the 'entertained' they probably thought we were a bug in their beer) the locals in the small countryside pubs round Scotland and Ireland we didn't enjoy being one of the crowd. Pamela wanted to go to Bono's place, the O-bar at the Clarence hotel. It had opened a couple of years before and she had read about it, so we wandered off to the more glamorous bar. Usually not our style but what-the-heck, you only live once (this was before that phrase was shortened yolo).

Walking in there was a total contrast from the Temple Bar with its beer-soaked drunk boys wobbling around. More cocktail than beer, not that crowded, and with smart-looking people spread out around the round bar under the octagon-shaped dome. We were definitely not going to get any attention here – we probably looked like the cats among the ermines, two green- and one black eyed – but somehow our more relaxed behavior, in contrast to the stiff uptight women we saw in there, drew the men to us. We tried to tag down a notch – singalong and armwrestling didn't seem like the proper thing here – but we couldn't restrain from waving our arms and laugh out loud while we chatted to anyone that wanted to listen.

Just as we had entered the bar my eyes spotted a tall man with wild brown hair, looking like a young Jim Morrison in The Doors (come to think of it – never was an old Jim Morrison in the Doors). Picture before you the photos of him, where he is bare chested, looking both suggestively and bold into the camera. This one had a perfectly shaped face just like him, the same kissable lips and bedroom eyes, but with a shirt on. A real-life Adonis. Somehow I was drawn to him - it was like magnetism in there. Before I knew it we were standing next to each other. In the way he grabbed me, like a predator that got its claws in his prey, I knew he had already taken notice of me. He bought me a drink before any of the other men around us had a chance to make their move, and thereby I had the 'hands-off, she's taken'-sign on my back. He was funny, charming, extremely full of life and absolutely GORGEOUS! When he asked me to come with him to another bar a couple of hours later I just said bye-bye to my friends, totally forgetting how irritated I had been with them disappearing on me (or maybe a way of getting even?), and walked off with him.

* * * * * * * * * * * * * * * * * * *

To: Andrea Hunter 2014-08-16 10:13
From: Gemma Littleton
Subject: Re: Re: Re: Re: Re: Re: Re: Re: Dwayne

Andrea,

Another sleepless night spent going over and over this mess trying to make some sense of it all. Dwayne did not stay here last night - he said he was going to stay at his mum and dads. He is coming home later this morning and I will be waiting for him with a long list of questions that I want answers to. I will lock the door and hide the key so he cannot run away like he always does. I know him well and he will be desperate at this point as he can see his life falling apart. It will be interesting to hear what lies he will come out with today. He cannot stand being questioned probably because he cannot give truthful answers. He is a pathological liar and always has been. Should we be surprised at the way Dwayne has turned out bearing in mind he has been brought up by 2 parents who clearly think it is acceptable to cheat and lie your way through life.

Andrea - if it makes you feel any better I have had the "what you don't know won't hurt you" line from Ellen as well. She said it to me once when I asked her something about Dwayne. I should have realized then what they were all capable of.

Where do we go from here? Are you going to tell your sons that you and Dwayne are not together? Like you say, it is important that they remain in contact with their Dad however much of an arsehole he is!! They should not be affected by all of this shit that's going on. Anyway would you want your sons brought up with Dwayne's morals - look at what he has already taught Sebastian -

yes Sebastian it is totally acceptable to have affairs and lead a double life. It upsets me so much to think that Dwayne has had to tell Sebastian to lie to me.

An alarm bell starts ringing in my head. Is she trying to convince me to not try to sort things out with Dwayne? I can't think of any reason to do so but I don't want her to tell me that.

As for the pictures in the house and in Dwayne's room... no wonder we never visited Ellen and Paul un-announced. Dwayne always rang to say we were going over. Once we were passing and I suggested popping in for a coffee - Dwayne pulled the car over and rang his mum to tell her we were coming (we were 1 minute away from the house). I wondered at the time why he would do that - now I know, so Mr and Mrs Honesty could rearrange their pictures!! I don't know about you but as the shock of all this is wearing off very slightly I am beginning to get angry and I mean SERIOUSLY angry. Do you want me to let you know what happens today? Come on Andrea admit it - you cannot wait to hear what bullshit is going to pour out of Dwayne's mouth now. Do you think it can get any worse, is there more to come? Was he leading a treble life?!!

Try to have a good day - I'm going swimming now to try and lose some of this anger.

Gemma

Try to have a good day? I'm sitting in the grass next to a children's playground. In the distance I can see the football field where Alexander is warming up for an important game in a football cup. Normally I would text Dwayne and let him know about the game, how the team and Alexander's shape was, he would text me back with good-luck wishes to his son and I would let him know about every goal in the game. Now I just feel empty. A part of me is hoping that Gemma will give him a really hard time but the fact that I can't do anything from a distance is making me emotionally drained.

SIX

Johnny O'Reilly

Johnny O'Reilly was his name. Not Adonis. His name is the only one in this book that is not changed. He was like a fantasy figure from the start.

After leaving the O-bar we went to a couple of bars that I hadn't a clue of what they were called, where they were situated or what the interior looked like – I only had eyes for Adonis. Sorry: Johnny O'Reilly. I was mesmerized, and glued to his lips. When one of his friends called and asked him to join a party, he asked if I wanted to come along. NOTHING could have stopped me. And since I was still glued to his lips it would have been difficult for him to leave without extreme pain and blood loss. I jumped in a cab with him and off we went.

The party was in a neighborhood with enormous, posh houses. It was full on, with people everywhere. Everyone seemed to know Johnny O'Reilly and looked like they wanted a bit of his beams. Including me. I had a hard time to keep track of him and as soon as I stopped to talk to someone he was off into the next room. He looked like he was floating. In hindsight I understand that he probably was high as a kite.

Eventually I got tired of his propelling from room to room, and grabbed him, pushed him in to one of the small lavatories, locked the door and whispered 'take me' into his ear. And boy – did he take me! He was a love-God!

Afterwards I was like a smitten kitten. We stumbled out, now me with a Jim Morrison-look with my usually straight hair completely tousled, and he propelled away again while I sank down on a couch, still purring.

I didn't take long before he came back with new energy (must have been drugs) and grabbed my hand and led me out of the house. We semi-ran hand-in-hand down the road to an even bigger house where he had trouble getting through the front door. It seemed he was lacking a key and when he started to climb up the pipes on the wall, and hauled himself through a small window that was partly open on the top floor, I was pretty sure that he was going to come out with some shining jewelry in his hands and that we were going to be arrested. But he just opened the door and gallantly lead me into the house.

In there was soft white carpets and what looked like expensive furniture. I was now convinced that he had broken into a wealthy person's house but I didn't care. He had his hands all over me, and those lips were on my neck, my ears, my shoulders, my...GOD!

He shoved me firmly into the kitchen and I actually had time to notice that it was made of dark walnut and shining black marble before he lifted me up on the kitchen island and laid me out like Jamie Oliver would have laid out a filet of lamb, smooching oil on it, sprinkle some herbs and rubbing it in with firm hands, tenderly licking the juicy and moist surface of the raw flesh before he sliced it up in... I completely exploded and was lost in space.

In the morning it turned out that he WAS living in that house. No one can be so familiar in a strangers house. And later that day, after we had a late breakfast, one of his friends came over with Love-God's – sorry I mean Johnny O'Reilly's - lost key. His friend didn't seem to be surprised that there was a woman in the bed so I probably wasn't the first one he had dragged home. They turned on some sports and cracked open a couple of beers and I realized that there wouldn't be any seconds or thirds actually, that afternoon.

Eventually I had to get myself together and get back to the hotel. We were heading back to Stockholm early the following morning and I hadn't let my friends know I was still alive and I expected to get a good whipping when I got back. I got Mr Love-God Adonis Johnny O'Reilly's email-address (without too much begging) and went out into the bright sunlight, totally clueless which direction Hardcore -

sorry Harcourt - lay. He wasn't much of a gentleman in the morning after, but what the heck — I had been in the Johnny O'Reilly heaven!

That was the last I saw of him.

When I got back to Sweden I was totally besotted with Johnny O'Reilly. I couldn't stop talking about him. He had gotten into my system with his relaxed and yet playful way. Although he felt unreachable really, and he for sure wasn't boyfriend material, I definitely wanted more. After a decent time of THREE DAYS — didn't want to seem too eager — I emailed him.

To: Johnny O'Reilly 98-07-28 16:56
From: Andrea Hunter
Subject: Svenska flicka!

Hello there my Irish climbing hero!
Back in Sweden after an enormously fun trip!! It is a bit hard to coordinate the thoughts now and actually work.
I really enjoyed myself Friday night - the image of your legs sticking out of the window is unbeatable. I got back to the hotel alright, but had bruises all over - must have been our toilet-session...
Det var en njutning att träffa dig! Puss & kram, Andrea

There. Throw in some Swedish and he is bound to be intrigued. Now let's hope for an answer. Soon.

Instead of an email from Adonis, I got several handwritten

letters (remember those that came in an envelope, with a cute little stamp of the Queen, a bird or some other colorful attribute and was delivered manually to your door?) from the young tour-guide slash musician in the making that we had guiding us in Scotland, Mark Hunter. He seemed to have fallen for me and was now sending me letter after letter with tapes of his music, asking for my opinion. I had only been keen on trying out my newly bought whisky-condoms and had absolutely no interest in him after that so I just ignored him. (Hasn't Cupid got a plan when sending out those arrows? Now it just seems a bit random I must say).

I was yearning day after day but no Johnny O'Reilly in the inbox. Days went into weeks and felt seriously ditched. Not even an answer. But somehow I knew he was only going to be a twinkling star inside my mind. (And sorry Mark, I didn't mean to hurt you. Hopefully you got loads of material to your lyrics and that you are famous now...).

* * * * * * * * * * * * * * * * * * * *

To: Gemma Littleton 2014-08-16, 14:53
From: Andrea Hunter
Subject: Re: Re: Re: Re: Re: Re: Re: Re: Re: Re: Dwayne

Gemma, as it sinks in more and more that it's been ME who has been 'the other woman' - not once, but twice as it's showed - I'm getting more and more numb. Can't even get angry with him - just think he is pathetic. I'm happy you are enough angry to not let him get out of this easy!! (Do get disproportionally VERY angry with Ellen & Paul for some reason).

To get your emails is the only thing that keep me sane right now and I'm ready to hear everything you want to tell me. I don't think you're gonna get the truth or answers from him though. It will be too easy for him to say he never loved me - when I'm not there and he has to look me in the eyes when he says it - and that he only pretended to have a relationship with me so that he could see the boys. Trust me - I have always made it clear to him that of course he would continue to see the boys even if we weren't together. That's why I can't figure out why he's continued the charade? Could be that it's because he always has wanted an option open - he seems terrified of getting tied down.

Of course I haven't got any proofs of us sleeping together while seeing you - he will continue denying that I think, but everything else there is photos of.

I do have a video that we made for fun of us having sex together (but I think we took it before he met you) - but since he seems a bit lost when it comes to dates and years you can try to use the knowledge of it as a way of getting him to admit him cheating - not only emotionally but also physically (he'll be so stressed he won't remember when we filmed it. Come to think of it - he was actually MARRIED then!!!!)

I haven't told the boys yet that we are not together any more and that he now lives with someone else. I don't have any problems in doing that but I don't want to risk that Dwayne still will be in his disappearing mode so that the boys feel that THEIR relationship has changed and they can't talk to him. I have always told the boys that it's better to tell about unpleasant things straight away since it gets worse if you don't - Jason lives after that but Alexander is acting a bit more like his father.

I'm trying desperately to think of a way to use this situation as an example without them starting to hate their father or (even worse :-) taking after him...

My mind is with you and I'm looking forward to hear from you again.

Andrea (with a Margarita headache today...)

SEVEN

Stockholm calling

A Friday morning in the middle of August, about one month after our Scotland-London-Ireland-trip, I got a phone call. I was getting ready to go to work, a bit later than usual.

"Hello, this is Tom." A voice with a heavy cockney accent in the other end.

"Oh hi! Are you up already? Did you get home alright last night? How's Richie?"

I was blabbering on, convinced it was one of the guys we were out with last night. Sophie, Pammie and I had met a bunch of English blokes that a Scottish guy I knew, Richie, had introduced us to the night before. Richie had a crush on me, but had finally got the message that I wasn't in to him after hearing about Johnny O'Reilly a million times. We had a great time in Bagpipers Inn, a Scottish pub in

Vasastan, the western part of the city. There had been so many new guys there so I had forgotten their names in an instant.

"No – this is Tom. Remember Dwayne? From The White Horse?"

I got very confused – how did he know about Dwayne and The White Horse? Had I talked about him last night?

"How do you know about that??" I asked puzzled.

"NO! We were at La Rueda. Can't you remember? You were quite into my friend."

Suddenly the penny dropped. The funny-looking older guy!

"OH! HI!! Sorry! I just woke up so I'm a bit dizzy! How are you?!"

"I'm fine. Who's Richie?"

"Oh, never mind, just a friend!"

I felt a bit embarrassed, just like your typical whimsy blonde who can't keep track of all men.

"I'm in Stockholm on business. Can we meet up for a drink tonight?"

"Sure! Of course! That will be lovely!"

I didn't dare to ask him if he was alone, or if by any chance Dwayne was with him. I was still flustered after the mixup – and getting REALLY late for work – so I just ended the conversation with a 'see you under the Mushroom at Stureplan at 5pm!' and rang off.

The Mushroom is like a big statue in the center of Stureplan, in the middle of Stockholm. If you are going to meet up with anyone in the city – a new date, an old boyfriend, a girlfriend – you always met up under the Mushroom. Currently they were doing some kind of renovation of it so half of it was hidden behind a plank.

As I jumped off the bus and walked down Kungsgatan – King Street in Swedish – I felt a flutter of thrill and nervousness. Could it be that Dwayne was going to be there as well? I wouldn't mind seeing him again, but I wasn't that keen on having a drink with that Tom-guy. He was quite old, half my size, and I hadn't a clue what we could talk about.

I had called Sophie for support. I didn't want to risk that Tom had any ideas in mind about him and me hitting it off. She was going to join us later.

The sun was shining after a week of drizzling summer rain. Stockholm was buzzing with life again now that people had come back from their summer-visits and it was Friday in basically the first proper working week. Expectation was in the air.

As I rounded the corner and got a full view of the Mushroom my heart sank. There stood that tiny grey-haired man. Alone.

I managed a smile and a wave, but before I could raise my voice and say 'hi' HE stepped out from behind the plank. HIM. Mr Gene Paul Newman Brando! With the widest smile I've ever seen. I literally jumped a couple of feet up in the air and my heart did a big rush from down the basement and ended in a somersault. My God! It was like getting struck by lightning – I was completely filled by

fireworks. I walked straight past ¯om and into Dwayne's
open arms and we kissed for what seemed like ages.

* * * * * * * * * * * * * * * * * * *

Sunday August 17th, 2014

The weekend continues and I don't hear a single word
from Gemma. Or Dwayne for that matter. What had
happened over there? Had she flipped out and killed him?
Or dug a big hole in the basement and thrown him in it?
Like in 'Silence of the lambs'. Or tied him to the bedpost,
and cut his dick off. I'm sure there is a movie with that
scenario.

On the Sunday morning I walk over to my parents house.
We are living in the same neighborhood and over the years
they have been helping me with the boys, as I have been
living as a single mum, even if I haven't been feeling as
one. Now they are sitting in their beautiful, flowery
garden, reading the morning paper on their veranda - built
by my father, sharing the different parts of the paper in a
habitual manner. They have always loved Dwayne. Him
being charming, funny and easy-going. Now it feels like
I'm about to break their hearts.
"Can you listen to me for a bit. And if the boys come over
we change the subject. What I am about to tell you the

boys don't know anything about yet, okay?"

I definitely have their attention now. Sometimes that can be a bit hard when breaking in on their morning routine.

"Last week I got an email from a woman claiming to be Dwayne's girlfriend. And it turns out that she is. They started dating when I was pregnant with Alexander. And more - he was married when we met. To another woman. He has had a second wife. And Dwayne's parents, and Sebastian, know about this."

I can see how the information eats its way into their brains. How the digestion starts but it's not easily processed. More like dry rye-bread than mashed potatoes.

"What??!" my mother finally says.

"Are you sure?" says my father. "Have you spoken to Dwayne?".

"No. Right now I have only had an email conversation with that woman. Gemma."

"So, it might not be true?" my father continues hopefully. "Can it be some crazy woman..."

"Dad - I'm sure" I break him off, thinking that our minds definitely work in the same way. That had been my first reaction as well.

"..." my mother mouths and looks shellshocked.

We sit in silence for a bit, and then they simultaneously say:

"Well, you have been apart for long times..."

"DON'T say it!" I burst out. "DON'T! Don't suggest that it is understandable that he has another girlfriend just because we have been in a long-distance relationship! I have also

68

been in one and I have been able to keep my knickers on! And the fact that he has also had a WIFE that I didn't know about, being married when we met AND when we made both Jason and Alexander - you have to understand that this is out of the ordinary! He is a really ugly fish!" (Sorry - Swedish expression. Like a pike or a shark swimming among the cute little Nemos).

My parents look a bit ashamed. Definitely thinking that I am right but also that I am wrong, that this wouldn't have happened if we had seen each other more often. I doubt that. Gemma had been there but that hadn't stopped him.

My mother starts attacking the problem from another angle.

"I can't understand why Ellen and Paul never said anything. How could they let you stay in the dark?"

"Well, according to Dwayne, Paul never does something without permission from Ellen. And Ellen seems to think that it is better to not know about bad things."

"I could never do that" my mother says firmly. "If Erik would have taken home someone else than Petronella I would have told her!".

Erik is my five year younger brother, who's gone steady with his Petronella for ages.

"Would you? Really? Even if it meant you were never going to see him again? Your own son?"

My mother hesitates. Touché.

"I definitely would have tried to convince Erik to do the decent thing anyway."

"And if he would have answered 'stay out of my business,

mum'?"

Sounds like something my brother could have answered, and it wouldn't surprise me if that is what Dwayne had said to his mother, and maybe added: 'think about the boys, maybe you wouldn't see them again'.

My mother humpfs and says:

"Anyway, I don't think Erik could have done a thing like that."

Well, now she is right. He wouldn't. He is a much too decent and nice person to do something so evil.

"What are you going to do?" my mother finally asks.

My father is silent, but judging by the tormented look on his face I'm guessing he is thinking about the boys and how they will react. Or maybe he is wondering what will happen with the steady income of fine whiskey that Dwayne always brings when he comes over. I seem to have lost the ability to read peoples minds.

"I don't know" I say. "Wait to see what happens next?"

Monday comes and goes and still no sign of life. I am like a robot at work, doing all the tasks mechanically, but with my mind somewhere else. The slow summer mode has been changed into the start of the more hectic period, both giving me the opportunity to think about something else but also interfering me in the processing of 'what-to-do-next'.

On the Tuesday a life sign finally arrives.

To: Andrea Hunter 2014-08-19, 10:00
From: Gemma Littleton
Subject: Re: Re: Re: Re: Re: Re: Re: Re: Re: Re: Re: Dwayne

Andrea, this is such a hard email to write. Dwayne and I have spent the last 3 days going over this mess. We have talked/screamed/shouted/cried. I am emotionally drained.
The outcome is that we are staying together. I know you must think I am crazy but I cannot imagine my life without him in it.

She must be in the denial phase. Surely.

He has been with me through so much, both good and bad. I have to face up to the truth, put it behind me and move on. Only time will tell if we have made the right choice. I don't want to hurt you by telling you things you don't need to know and I cannot take anymore pain.

She is not only in denial. She must be brainwashed? Or braindrained. How does she think she can ever trust that man? What has he said to her? And what does she mean by not 'telling me things I don't need to know'?

I am so unbelievably sad and sorry about all that has gone on. We must both find strength from somewhere and carry on.

Maybe she is part of some religious sect? Forgive anything and forget everything.

Dwayne still wants to see his sons in the future and I know you would not stand in the way of that.

EXCUSE ME? Is she the one who should give me this information?

I know I am probably going to regret the choice that I have made

YES YOU WILL!!!

- after all a leopard never changes its spots.

NO HE DOESN'T!

Only time will tell.

What do you mean 'time will tell'?! I can tell you now - NO, YOU ARE NOT MAKING THE RIGHT CHOICE!

You are in my thoughts.
Gemma

FUCK.

Well I certainly don't want him. She can have him. But don't we have to talk first before they can just move on? Hasn't he have to face up to me? And say that he is sorry? All of a sudden I just want all of this to be over. I don't reflect that I might be in some kind of a phase myself.

EIGHT

Knock-knock-knockin' on heaven's door

Dwayne, Tom and I went to Sturehof, a trendy bar/restaurant just next to the Mushroom. Interior of white tiles, marble and gold details – very late 90's – with Gin & Tonic as their signature drink, a wink to the ironic generation which we belonged to. Dwayne and I couldn't keep our hands off each other, and I felt thrilled to have this big, strong and handsome man by my side while sipping the juniper-scented drink from a tall, slim glass.

When Sophie joined us an hour later the sipping turned into more of a gulping. We decided to leave the minimalist designed bar with its smart dressed customers for a more common one further away from the posh Stureplan, and ended up at a packed bar in one of the side streets. There Sophie and I introduced the innocent Londoners to our brilliant new twist of Tequila Knock. The original one is just a shot of tequila which you put the palm of your hand over, knock the shot glass hard on the bar counter and drink. We had developed that recipe:

1. order a shot of Tequila Gold
2. stand in front of each other and stare into your drinking partners eyes for several seconds
3. simultaneously smack each others foreheads with the right palm of your hand
4. drink the shot in one gulp
5. grab your partners head and shake it vigorously
6. get knocked out

After showing how it should be done I turned to Dwayne and did it with him, but we had problems keeping our hands where they should be so Sophie took on the task to show Tom the proper way.

Sophie never do things halfheartedly – especially not when a bit drunk.

Little Tom tumbled helplessly backwards when she smacked him in the head without warning after forgetting the obligatory staring in the eyes. She roared 'DRINK' when he seemed a bit confused (along with everyone else in the bar), sitting on the floor holding what was left of his shot, and then she grabbed his head shaking it madly while lifting him up, his little feet dangling in the air.

Dwayne and I bent over double with laughter – it was absolutely the most funny thing we've ever seen (this was before everything was filmed and published on Youtube, Facebook, Instagram and God knows what). Tom's eyes were rolling in his eye sockets like the numbered balls in the Lotto wheel and every bit of him participating in the conversation that evening disappeared. (He never became the same after that bar-round. I don't know if his brain got some serious damage or if it was the fact that a tall slim blonde, even if originating from the vikings, had shaken him like a baby, but as I heard of it he disappeared from the social life when coming back to London and buried himself in cocaine and other heavy drugs).

After that the evening turned into a blur. I remember various bars, dancing and sweaty, aroused snogging with Dwayne, but eventually I dragged him with me into a cab and headed off to my small studio in Råsunda, just off central Stockholm.

We did have sex that night. Too drunk both of us, and forgetting everything that had something to do with contraceptives. I remembered I was thinking 'sod it – this is now my boyfriend' before wrapping my legs around him, like a way of justifying myself. Practicing safe sex in the Russian roulette manner – pointing the revolver in another direction just as you're squeezing the trigger.

Imagine – this man having unprotected sex with a Swedish girl in her bed was actually six months, give or take a couple of months, into his second marriage (if you have forgotten to do the maths), and the girl that was in his arms was under the impression that she, with a little help from destiny - who's name apparently was Tom - had just come together with the man of her dreams...

* * * * * * * * * * * * * * * * * * * *

Tuesday August 19th, 2014

Okay. I need to get in control. Make a list. What has to be done now?
1. Get in contact with Dwayne.
2. Tell the boys.
3. ?

I don't know what the third step would, or should, be. Make him suffer? Plan a revenge? Continue life as before? See a shrink?
I text Dwayne.

I will call you later today or this week so we can sort out the economic details. Make sure you answer.

And I let him know that if he doesn't answer I will contact the Swedish authorities to get them to chase him for money. He wouldn't like that. Psychopath or not.

To: Gemma Littleton 2014-08-19 12:00
From: Andrea Hunter
Subject: The future

Thanks for letting me know Gemma. I have sent a text to Dwayne that I will contact him this week about the economic arrangements concerning the boys. I'm not sure if he has had a special phone handling our relationship (and has now thrown it away or keeping it off) so I don't know if he has got the text. He and I have to sort the terms out by Monday. After that I let the Swedish authorities handle him instead.

I'll tell the boys in a couple of weeks - I want them to start school after the summer-break and go back to normal routines first. And the first time they come over to London after this I'll probably go with them so that they can see that their mum and dad can face each other. I don't want them to start disliking him for hurting me. I'll let you know when, so that Dwayne doesn't have to lie about it. I'll make him pay for a very VERY luxurious room for me in a nice hotel (without him in it of course...).

I don't think you are crazy. It's a human reaction after such a shock, and after several days of emotional turmoil anyone would want to get back to normal tracks.

Secretly I'm hoping that she is getting the subtext that she doesn't know what she is doing right know, that she eventually will come to her senses and throw him out. The thing he has done is so wrong in every way, and anyone that is capable of that shouldn't have the benefit of having someone by his side.

Thank you for contacting me so this charade didn't have to go on, and if you further down the line still want to have that drink and throw one (or more people) off the Putney Bridge I'm all up for it! Andrea

I am quite sure that we will meet up eventually.

NINE

Mr Tall - Dark - Stranger
becomes Mister Right

We woke up late that afternoon and dreamily started making love (my version of it – his was probably: having sex) again. I found out that he

- was about to turn 35 (perfect – had hopefully done enough of roaming around and should be ready to settle down)
- had a son age 9 named Sebastian, who lived mainly with the mother
- had divorced his wife when his son was only one
- he'd married her because it was something he hadn't done before and it seemed like a fun thing
- the divorce felt like a failure but he didn't miss her

- his ex-wife, aka Sebastian's mum, was an american woman and also a mad cow that had taken their son to the States the first year after their divorce so he hadn't seen much of him when he was young
- she was now back in London and living with one of his old friends (the guy she was together with when Dwayne had snatched her) and was pregnant with him

Good. She wouldn't be a threat then. Ex-wives, and especially a mother to a mans child, could always be a possible 'getting-back-together-for-child-and-old- times-sake'-thing.

That long weekend in Stockholm Dwayne and I were in each others arms 24/7. We hardly got out of bed – poor Tom had to loop around town on his own – and we only got up to get ourselves something to eat or drink. (I did not find out how he preferred his tea on this trip. I served him a huge cup of lukewarm milky tea – the way I liked it – and he drank it politely. Obviously the deceiving begun already then. He likes his tea really strong, screaming hot, and with a tiny splash of milk which I found out much later).

The morning after Dwayne and Tom had gone back to London my mobile rang.
I was currently working with a former stuntman who had taken on the Swedish version of the BTCC – the STCC, the Swedish Touring Car Championship. I was his right hand (wo)man and every second week we were covering the

races in different parts of Sweden. Every other week I edited the British version of the race that came to us in a full version and I cut it down into a 30 minute show.

"Hi baby" an English voice came from the other end.

"Who is this?" I asked suspiciously, damaged from the cock -up when Tom called, and afraid to make any mistakes if it was one of the BBC-producers that had somehow taken on a non formal tone.

"It's Dwayne!" I heard Dwayne say with both surprise and a 'I can't believe you don't remember who I am'-voice that I had some sympathy for since I'd been shagging him all weekend. He had probably never been treated like that before. But most certainly had been in the opposite situation...

"Oh hi darling! I miss you madly! When are you back?"

A week after Dwayne's visit I finally got an answer to my email to Adonis. I had almost forgot about him. It felt weird. Dwayne had effectively wiped out every bit of lust I might have felt for any other man.

To: Andrea Hunter 98-08-31, 02:34
From: Johnny O'Reilly
Subject:

Hi Andrea, sorry I've taken so long to reply. Tell me – I'd love to know – what does 'Det var en njutning att träffa dig' and 'Puss & kram' mean? Both phrases sounds very salacious.
All the best. Johnny O'Reilly

Well, TOO LATE Johnny! I have found Mr Right. You will now never know what it means! It was good that I had found Mr Right. The 'All the best' wasn't exactly what you wanted to hear from a man that you fancied and that you hoped were in to you.

I also got an email from Scottish Richie. A very dramatic one.

To: Andrea Hunter 98-09-02 11:20
From: Richard Winston
Subject: Goodbye

Dear Andrea, I may never see you again.
My account has to lose 10 people and I am the newest to my account. I will be told on Monday. If I do not have any job I will be flown back to Scotland the same evening without further notice. I do not want to leave Sweden. This is a nightmare.
Last weekend I was in Scotland. All my friends say hello to you.
Take care
Rich

I never heard from him again. He must have been put on that plane. Poor fella', but I didn't give it a second thought - my mind was elsewhere.

Dwayne and I spoke and texted each other several times a day. I felt abstinence if not being in contact after a couple of hours. My whole body was buzzing and bubbling when I thought of him – which was all the time – and we laughed and got each other aroused over the phone. We had the same kind of humor and we knew exactly what to say and text to get each other turned on and longing for more. And he had the body that could match mine. We seemed to be made for each other!

Now, when you are enamored it is like a state of illness. Both mental and physical. And it is definitely based on tricks that your brain does to you. So you don't really have to meet the object of your affection to feel that you are connected, and everything that object says is translated into exactly what you want to hear when passing through your ears, swirling through the fluffy pink clouds that are currently taking position in your head, before it ends up in your dwindling cerebral cortex.

Eventually you want to meet though. To get some refilling of the fluffy pink before it fades out. More than a month later came the good news.

"I'll see you tomorrow!"
"What?! You've got to be kidding me?!"
"Ha ha – no – I'm coming over with some of my lads, they are very keen to come to Stockholm."
I wasn't surprised. I could only imagine what Dwayne had told his friends about Stockholm. And Swedish women. 'Great partying with great frisky blondes!'. Sophie and I had probably done a good thing for the weekend city tourism to Stockholm by fulfilling every wet dream any Englishman could have about Swedish girls.

"And I'm longing to get back in between your legs again baby!"

Thank God for that – I wasn't in the party mood – I was in love and I just wanted to be in the arms of my man again.

"When are you coming?"

"Several times I hope" he said with a suggestive voice. "I call you when we are in town!"

'Call you in town' meant different things to me and Dwayne. This was just the first of uncountable let down expectations for me when it came to him. I should have known, but – fluffy pink does magic for your judgement. It simply erases everything that is not positive.

To me it meant 'call you as soon as I get off the plane and put my foot on Swedish ground my sweet darling love of my life'. To Dwayne it was more like 'sometime when I am in Stockholm this trip with my friends I will call you so we can have sex'.

When the clock passed eleven at night the date of their arrival I was pissed off. Where the hell was he?

A half hour before midnight he called. Very drunk, in a splendid mood, from one of the popular bar and dancing places in town – Biblos – and shouted 'come here baby!'

I on the other hand had longed to put my arms around him, had waited for hours to finally see him again, with my body smothered in soft body lotion, hair washed and brushed to perfection, with silky underwear and ready for bed – with him – and not in the mood at all for drinking

84

and partying.

"No, I'm too tired" I said a bit frosty. "You have fun and I'll see you tomorrow."

"Oh" came his surprised response. "I didn't realize it was that late?"

He sounded a bit disappointed when we hung up. But not too let down. I started to get a bit nervous. Biblos. Like a big meat-market. Dancing, drinking and loads of temptation. Suddenly I rushed up – 'who the heck am I? Sleeping beauty waiting to be kissed??'

I realized that if you want something you have to grab it. I called a cab and then Sophie, who also had been waiting for a phone call – eager to meet some more funny Londoners to shake around, and off we went to town.

At Biblos (16 years later, a Diesel jeans clothes store) we met up with Dwayne and his lads: Crazy Carter who always managed to get thrown out of every bar he entered, Toothless Tim who was...toothless – or rather lacking teeth on the right side of his upper jaw, Rick with no special features at all – just your average guy, and of course – Mr Destiny: Tom. I felt so special when I could just walk straight into the arms of the most handsome man in the bar and kiss him. I imagined that every girl in there wondered who I was that took possession of the tall dark stranger they'd been lurking on, and after three dances just took him by the hand and lead him home.

* * * * * * * * * * * * * * * * * * *

Wednesday August 20th, 2014

To: Andrea Hunter 2014-08-20, 18:00
From: Gemma Littleton
Subject: Re: The future

Hi Andrea,
*I hope you manage to sort out arrangements amicably - I will do
the best I can to make sure Dwayne faces up to his responsibilities.*

Oh. She has suddenly taken on a much more formal tone.

*He told me once that he was in trouble with the Swedish
authorities regarding maintenance for Jason (at that time I only
knew about one son) and could possibly have gone to
prison. Probably another one of his warped stories. Do you think
he is a frustrated gangster - he seems to tell a lot of lies involving
criminal activity!! Of course we will meet up - how could we not
after all we've been through. Stay in a hotel with a good bar and
we will go through every drink on the cocktail list. He can pay for
that as well. If I start plotting revenge on the Peterson family you
must stop me drinking !!*
*Keep in contact - I know I will be relying on you more to tell me
what's going on than Dwayne......*
I am here if you need to talk.
Take care.

That was that. One week has passed and a 16 year relationship is just wiped away. And I still haven't spoken to Dwayne.

How is she able to go on with that man? What has he said to her? He must have said something to make her believe that it is possible to continue with him. But what? In the past he has always slagged his old girlfriends off, that they have been mad, stupid cows or crazy bitches, including Sebastian's mum. She just wanted money for this and that. I suddenly feel a lot more understanding towards her if it ended between them in a similar way. It wouldn't surprise me.

TEN

"Oops – I think I was a bit late"

The morning after started late, and just like the mornings from Dwayne's previous visit we were staying in bed, kissing, cuddling and making love. This morning turned out a little bit differently though.

I was sitting on top of him when the phone rang.

"Don't answer" Dwayne groaned.

"'Course not" I moaned back, continuing the slow ride.

The phone just rang and rang, and then the answering machine clicked on.

By that time it was mostly common to have one with a little tape that started rolling and you could hear who was talking, not just something taking a message in cyberspace. I must have been deaf when listening to previous messages because now Sophie's voice came out ridiculously loud in the little room where Dwayne and I were getting sweaty under the covers.

"Heeellooo? Are you there?"

She started giggling.

"What are you do-o-o-ing?"

"Are you making looooooove?"

She chatted away and never seemed to stop. The slow ride had now turned into more of a trot as Dwayne's lips got tighter and tighter. He turned me around, grabbed my legs and seemed to get more focused.

"Can you aaaaaanswer?"

"Are we gonna meet up today or what?"

"Or shall I just get back to bed?"

"What ARE you doing?"

A salty pearl of sweat dropped from Dwayne's forehead and landed in my eye making me blink frantically as we now went into a full gallop, me trying to hold on for dear life with my legs wrapped around him.

"I'm nearly there" he hissed between his tight lips. "You?"

"Yeah" I lied, suddenly feeling it a bit too absurd to lay there listening to Dwayne panting in one ear and my best friend chattering in the other.

"YO-HOOOOOOOOOOO!!!!!"

Sophie suddenly shouted out loud just as Dwayne's eyes rolled back in his head, and he pulled out and sank down heavily next to me. It got totally quiet in the room. Sophie had rang off.

"I think I was a bit late there" he said.

"I hope not" I answered, "I'm ovulating."

My periods came like clockwork, always 28 days between them. I had checked my calendar when Dwayne told me he was coming over – I didn't want to risk any hanky-panky being stopped by menstruation – so I knew I was just in between periods. Just in between. In heat. I knew my body well enough to also know I always got more sexually on fire those days in the middle. The evolution certainly knew how to make sure we reproduced.

"Really?" I asked doubtfully. I'd never had this type of conversation before. "Were you really late? In that case we might have to do - something??"
He knew I wasn't on the pill because, although drunk as I were the first night we had sex the previous visit, I had managed to let him know that.
"Nah, I probably made it."
He leaned forward and started talking into my belly.
"Hello? Is there somebody in there?"
And we both started giggling.

I called Sophie afterwards.
"Well, you were KIND OF interfering when you called. If something has happened YOU will be the Godmother!"
"Of course I will be! What? Were you at it? How funny!"

In the evening we all met up at a little french restaurant. Dwayne was joking when I got my glass of red wine.
"Are you sure you should drink that" nodding meaningly at my stomach.

"Ha HA" I answered and took a big gulp just to prove my point. Of course I wasn't pregnant. That would be too weird.

He continued teasing me, and constantly put a protective hand on my belly and kept saying 'be careful' as soon as I drank of the wine.

When we came out into the wet and windy October streets, from the warm and cosy restaurant, the wine suddenly rushed up to our heads and Sophie and I got into one of our singing moods. Song of the weekend was 'You're just too good to be true' by Frankie Valli. This year it was out in a remake by Lauryn Hill, and we kept on singing that same song, driving the guys mad.

I was now singing it directly to Dwayne and I meant every word of it:

"You're just too good to be true
Can't take my eyes off of you
You'd be like heaven to touch
I wanna hold you so much'

I felt so lucky! A big, strong, handsome AND confident man was mine!

'A long last love has arrived
And I thank God I'm alive
You're just too good to be true
Can't take my eyes off of you'

He was really too good to be true. (A different context with the 'true'-bit now that I know what I know...).

He kissed me (probably to get me to shut up) and squeezed my tits.

"Oh – they have started to get bigger!"

The last day of their trip the weather had changed. A high pressure had moved in and had forced away the gloomy rainy clouds and now the sun was shining. Chilly nordic winds was foreboding that the autumn was just around the corner. Dwayne and I had after 48 hours finally gotten out of bed and gone into the city where we had planned to meet up with everyone at the Soap Bar, the newest addition to the Stureplan bar-jungle, for a final bar-round before the guys entered their flight home. Dwayne and I were strolling slowly hand-in-hand alongside the quay, sun in our faces and sadness in our minds.

"I don't want you to leave" I said and managed a smile.

"I don't want to leave" he answered.

We sat down on a little bench just by the water and watched the sun glitter in the blue water, me on his lap. I felt so small in his arms (and let me tell you – it takes a lot of man to make me feel that) and I tried to inhale the masculine scent of his neck to really store it in my memory bank.

"When are we going to see each other again Dwayne?"

"Soon."

I settled with that. He was going to take charge of this. He said we were going to see each other soon and so we would. I didn't realize that 'soon' was his standard answer to almost anything... but hey - I was over the moon.

To: Pete Roderick 98-10-06, 15:52
From: Andrea Hunter
Subject: Yohooo!!!

I'm so in love!!!! It IS raining in the desert!!! Flooding actually! Dwayne came over from London again this weekend and I am absolutely up in the clouds!!!!!! AAAAAAAHH!! There IS someone for me!!!! Forgot the feeling but now it's really clear! Life is MMMMMMMMMMMMMMMMMMMMMM!! Puss & kram, Andrea

ELEVEN

The line that changes the world

When Dwayne went back to London again I didn't miss him at first. I was so filled up by him and so extremely in love that I felt I was ready to explode. I just wanted to stay in that bubble for a while, and re-live the weekend in my mind, over and over again. I didn't change the sheets when he left. I inhaled the scent of his hair from the pillow he had laid his head on, and a T-shirt that he left behind smelled of his body and the aftershave he had worn - Gío - and some detergent I didn't know from before. Inside I felt electric and I was aware of every inch of my body. My skin was rosy and soft, my groin tingled, my nipples felt sensitive and my face was glowing. I was definitely in love.

We continued to speak and text several times a day. Funny, erotic and longing texts. How we missed each other, and what we were going to do next time we met. We just didn't know when that would be.

I had another trip planned with Sophie in a months time, this time to Singapore. One of our best friends, Mika, had moved there with her husband, their daughter – my Godchild – and their newborn son, and we had promised to come and see her. We were flying via London, and started talking about staying some extra hours in London before we continued to Singapore, so Dwayne and I at least could meet each other before too long.

The day when my period was supposed to come it didn't. Since my body was filled with butterflies of love I wasn't surprised, I knew the body could play tricks on you when something was out of the ordinary, but when day 29 and 30 came and went with no signs of Little Red Riding Hood I got nervous. This had never happened before. I told Dwayne but he just said 'relax, it's only two days, it'll come' but I knew that with the nervousness I felt I needed to get a pregnancy test to be calmed. The period could come to a halt if you worried or stressed about something, and now I definitely needed to calm myself down. I decided to take the test on the 31st morning if it hadn't arrived during the night.

At the crack of dawn I was a wreck. I had tossed and turned the whole night, and hardly gotten any sleep. At six o'clock I realized that I just had to get it over with. I got up, drank two big glasses of water, went in to the tiny bathroom and turned on the light. The yellowish light reflecting in the turquoise tiles got me nauseous. My hands were shaking as I opened the package and took the little test-stick out. I read the instructions at least three times. 'When the blue line to the left is visible, the test is complete. If a second blue line is visible to the right you are pregnant' was the basic message. I tried to breathe normally. The yellow lighting, lack of sleep and nervousness made me feel ill. I put the tester down and started weeing.

By the time it took for me to finish the wee and hold the test-stick up in front of my face two blue lines started to visualize simultaneously. No 'okay-lets-keep -the-tension-going', or 'let's see where this will take us'. No, it was an instant answer. Speaking out loud. YES. YOU. ARE. PREGNANT. With a man you've known for less than 3 months and just met on 3 different occasions. Living in another country (AND HE IS JUST MARRIED - BUT NOT TO YOU! we could have added, but we didn't know that then, did we). I got up from the loo, went straight to the phone and made the call. The main, important, necessary first one.
"Sophie - you are going to be a Godmother."

* * * * * * * * * * * * * * * * * * *

I start to think that it actually has to be something wrong with him. Like mentally wrong. Could he be a psychopath? Or have a borderline personality?

I start googling "Psychopath" and immediately find a test on Wikipedia with 20 questions. If the patient or criminal (!) gets more than 30 out of 40 points he or she has passed the limit.

Ah – let's do this!

1 point for every answer that is accurate. 2 points if it matches very well.

Question 1: Well spoken/shallow charming.

Yes! 2 points!

Question 2: Grandiose self appreciation.

Hmm, 1 point?

Question 3: Need for excitement, easily bored.

He certainly has his ups and downs, but so do I. 1 point.

Question 4: Pathological liar.

OH YES!!! NO DOUBT! Can I give more than two points?

Question 5: Deceiving/manipulative.

Deceiving yes, but manipulative? Maybe I just haven't understood it? 1 point. Must not exaggerate.

Question 6: Lacks regret and remorse.

Well he isn't acting enough remorseful. 1 point.

Question 7: Flat, shallow emotional life.

Yes. Definitely. 2 points.

Question 8: Cold, lacking empathy.

Hmm, tricky. When it comes to me it seems like he's not able to understand me and my feelings, but when it comes to the boys I've always been able to hear in his voice that he can understand the feelings of a sad little boy. But I've always thought that he must have an emotional on/off-switch. How could he otherwise spend so much time away from his boys? How can anyone just bury themselves into work and forget what's really important? 1 point and then I'm being nice.

Question 9: Parasitical lifestile.

Maybe that Gemma is rich and he is dependent on her? And he has the top floor of his parents house. But he always says that he is paying them. Paying them to keep quiet maybe? 1 point.

Question 10: Lack of self control, easily awakened anger.

Well sometimes he could get irrationally angry with something that I thought was nothing. On the other hand I myself can be incredibly angry about something he wouldn't understand. And the medicine he takes for his high blood-pressure has calmed him down. As well as his erection. 1 point.

Question 11: Promiscuous and egoistic sex-life.

Didn't think he was promiscuous but what do I know apparently? Maybe it wasn't just me he was bonking while married? I must thank my lucky star that it was boys I got and not venereal diseases... Egoistic? Well he did his halfhearted attempts to make me happy in bed, and I could get crazily aroused with him, but he didn't have the patience to get me to climax. And didn't listen when I told him what I wanted. 'Want me to stop?' was his constant childish answer if I asked him to go slower, or be a bit softer. Both in traffic and in bed. 2 points.

Question 12: Early behavior problems (before age of 12).

Well according to his mum he drove her nuts. 2 points.

Maybe it's her fault? Threw him out of the house already at 16. At least that is what he said she did.

Question 13: Lacks realistic, longterm goals; acts short sightedly, and cannot plan longterm.

102 points!! At least. Okay – 2 then. Spot on anyway.

Question 14: Impulsive.

2 points. But isn't that something we can all be at times, especially when we are younger? He was more impulsive before, I wouldn't call him that now. I change it to 1 point.

Question 15: Lack of responsibility, as boss or parent.

T.W.O.P.O.I.N.T.S. Hmm. Sometimes he actually acts like he is responsible. Especially when it comes to the boys. But I have to do the work. 1 point.

Question 16: Doesn't take responsibility of his actions.

Well, there is no doubt about that. 2 points.

Question 17: Many short marriage-like relationships.

Well that was a tricky one. They are not short. Not the ones I know about anyway... But the fact that he has them at the same time must count for something? 1 point.

Question 18: Juvenile delinquent.

Don't really know. Wouldn't be surprised. But 0 points.

Question 19: New criminal actions while on parole.

Hmm. 0 points.

Question 20: Criminal diversity.

Eh, not that I know of anyway. 0 points.

Okay, let's see. 24 points. He doesn't qualify. On the other hand I would get 0 points, or maybe 1 or 2 if I stretch it. Clearly something must be a bit twisted in his head?

TWELVE

Number one on the list of things a man doesn't want to hear

Due to the time difference to England I had to wait another couple of hours before I called Dwayne. London is only one hour earlier but I was a bundle of nerves and I wanted to be sure that he would be awake and answer – I couldn't handle to get to the answering machine. I took the underground to work but instead of getting the bus the last bit I started walking. I passed the quay where Dwayne and I had sat hand-in-hand a couple of weeks before. The sun was shining like it had that day but now it was actually warmer, as the chilly northern winds had been replaced by some smooth southern ones.
I called him.

"Good morning baby!"

He sounded so cheerful and I felt dreadful. Jeez – how high is this on a list of '10 things a man does not want to hear from a girl he had sex with'.

"Are you sitting down?"

"Yeah, why? I'm in the car."

"I did a pregnancy test this morning."

"You're not pregnant."

"Yes, I am."

He started laughing.

Of all the reactions I had tried to predict, this was not one of them. And it felt good. He didn't panic or freak out.

"You're laughing Dwayne?! This is crazy! What are we going to do?"

"Sure it's mine?" he said, but with the same laughing voice, and it sounded like he wasn't expecting an answer. He knew the answer.

"Of course it's yours – I haven't been with anyone else since I met you."

Now – technically that wasn't true. I HAD been with another man since I met him. Johnny bloody O'Reilly. But that was months and months before and periods had come and gone several times since then. It was no doubt whatsoever that Dwayne's and my October-session had done the trick. I hadn't been with anyone else since I met Dwayne – in Stockholm. You don't have to be TOO honest.

* * * * * * * * * * * * * * * * * *

I text Dwayne.

Call me on my mobile.

Then I ad:

This is Andrea.

Nothing happens.

From Sweden.
In STOCKHOLM I might have to clarify.

I feel like I have the right mixture of humor and irony for him to dare to make the call but still nothing. How can he be so ignorant? And such a bloody coward. I wish I could just cut everything off with him and never hear from him again. But I can't. We have two boys together. While I try to figure out what to do next I finally get a life-sign from him a couple of hours later.

Hi Andrea sorry I missed your call and SORRY for the whole load of shit and upset I have caused to everybody Can we speak tomorrow evening pls I am putting money in your account tomorrow for you and the boys

After a couple of minutes I get another one.

Sorry Andrea x

I start to wonder if it really is him who sent the first one. Or her. Helping him to clear up this mess. It's his usual signature-texting with no dots or commas or question marks but he has suddenly started using capital letters which he hasn't used before in his texts. I answer him. I want him to know that I'm not sitting home crying after him.

Have an afterwork-thing tomorrow. Call you after if I'm sober enough. Or drunk enough.

The after-work-thing is with Ella. I want to let her in on the development of the story. It did really turn out worse than when we had first spoken about it. Ella just gasps as she hears me coolly pour out the details about Dwayne's deceit. I don't leave anything out. Strangely enough it fills me with a satisfaction that it wasn't just a simple, common affair. Makes me feel special and I like that, but I also feel weird for feeling that. I enjoy seeing her eyes get wider and wider. I finish with telling her that they had decided to continue together and that I still haven't spoken to him.

"How can you be so cool, Andrea? Aren't you sad? Or heartbroken? Or mad at least? What a bastard!"

I take a sip from the glass of champagne. I had chosen to meet in the T/bar at the Diplomat Hotel which has happy-hour every Thursday with half price on the expensive bubbles. I feel like I want to celebrate.

"When I first realized that he had fucked-me-up big time I wanted him to have a heartattack and just die so no one would find out. But now I think that it is good that it is out in the open, and we just have to move along from here. We will probably be as usual when we meet, you know - joking and chatting, not having sex of course, but just be parents to the boys. And maybe he has got something wrong in his brain to be able to pull off a thing like this. Maybe something in his childhood. It has always been hard for him to make a choice and make plans, he has just tagged along. And if he has a psychopath-streak there is nothing to do - you can never change them."

She looks at me with distrust.

"It surely must be something not right in his head. Jeez Andrea, you should want to tear his eyes out!"

"Well I might do. Maybe I am still in shock and will wake up soon, ha ha" I say as I finish my second glass of Moët. "Can we talk about you now instead? What has been going on in your life?"

A lot apparently...

When I leave Ella I don't feel like talking to Dwayne at all. I feel rebellious. Let him sweat for a bit before he is off the hook. He is probably very nervous about having to talk to me. And I realize that by not being sober I am probably a bit moody. On one hand I feel so incredibly angry and hurt and sad that there is a risk that I'm just going to scream and cry on the phone. And another side of me feel so cold and jolly at the same time that it will come out like his betrayal is nothing. I really feel like Dr Jekyll and Mrs Hyde.

I text him.

I call you tomorrow.

Better safe than sorry. Don't do anything irrational. I have no obligations to call him when I've said I will. He hasn't kept his promises, has he?

Friday August 22th, 2014

When the Friday comes I understand that I just have to get it over with. I'm a bundle of nerves and I keep going over and over in my head what we need to talk about. I feel mental. I am now so incredibly angry with him and at the same time deep frozen. In the morning I send him a text.

Call me before 3pm your time

When the phone rings at 2:45pm I have forgotten I have put it on silent for a meeting. I am talking to one of my colleagues in another part of the room when I suddenly start thinking of Dwayne and from a distance I can see that my phone lights up on my desk. Like a sixth sense. 'Sorry' I say to my surprised colleague and rush to get it.
"Hello?"
"Hi, it's me."

"Hi. Hold on, I just have to get a room."

Once again I'm sitting in the little conference room.

"So..."

I honestly don't know what to say. There are so many questions I want to ask, so much anger I want to let out and I don't know where to begin.

"Look, I'm sorry Andrea..."

"Well it is done now. We have to sort out the financial details around the boys."

Better to keep the conversation practical. After all I'm at work and I don't want to break down in pieces.

"Andrea - you know I always give you money, and make sure that you and the boys have enough."

"That isn't the problem - the problem is that you never do it on time, and I have to keep reminding you and..."

I'm winding myself up. All the frustration I have inside of me now explodes into a silly argument about things that doesn't matter really - not at this point anyway. He gets on his defensive and starts arguing back and after a couple of minutes of hard words I suddenly stop. All my anger just disappears and I just ask him the crucial question.

"Why Dwayne. Why?"

"I don't know Andrea."

He sounds lost.

"It just happened."

"But how did you think this would go on? You must have realized that eventually this would come out in the open??"

"It wasn't something I planned. I don't know Andrea! I keep different things of my life in different boxes in my head."

Nice. Now I'm in a box.

"And you were married when we met for Christ's sake Dwayne!"

"Yeah, but that was a mistake, it just lasted a year..."

"A YEAR?!!"

I go mad.

"A YEAR! You were married to her and living with her until you started dating Gemma! That is at least THREE years!!"

"But she wasn't home much, she was an air hostess..."

My God. He is really twisted. I wonder if SHE felt that their marriage was a mistake, and really only lasted for a year, or if she like me wondered where the closeness had gone, and if she also had called his mother and desperately tried to understand what he was up to, like I had done on his disappearing acts.

"Dwayne - you are crazy. Do you know I've actually done a test for you to see if you are a psychopath."

He starts laughing.

"How did I do?"

"You only scored 24 out of 40, so you don't qualify. But you are close. I bet there is some other mental or psychological disorder you've got. I'm going to keep looking."

"Ha, ha, you are so special."

"I know, but not special enough apparently..."

"No Andrea, I mean it. You are special."

He goes quiet.

"Dwayne?"

I suddenly hear that he sobs.

"Dwayne..."

"I'm so sorry Andrea. I have been all numb since all this came out, I haven't been able to feel anything. I didn't mean to hurt you..."
"Well you did Dwayne."

We sit in silence for a while. I can hear him sob quietly. Right now there isn't anything more to say.
"Much as I want to continue this conversation Dwayne, I think we need to end it here."
"But I don't want it to end!"
He sounds like an angry and upset little boy as his voice breaks into heavy sobs.
"Well, it has to."
....talk about a symbolic subtext...
He still sobs.
"Bye" I say.
"By-hy-e"
His voice sounds very distant. I can picture him in his car. His head bent down between his broad shoulders. I feel a maternal instinct take over. I want to comfort him. Say that it is not that bad and that everything will get better. But instead I hang up. I feel emotionally drained.
5 minutes later I get a text from him.
A one-letter word, saying everything:

X

PART 2.

THE RELATIONSHIP WITH
DWAYNE

THIRTEEN

Singapore Sling

On November 5th it was finally time for me and Sophie to go to Singapore, with a 9 hour stop in London.

"Make sure you and Dwayne talk properly now" Sophie said on the plane. "Don't just jump in the sack and start joking and kiss and cuddle like you usually do, you have some serious business you have to make a decision about" she continues firmly, having seen how Dwayne and I became in each others presence.

"Okay, we will talk about it."

That was the whole point with the long stop in London, and the reason she agreed on entertaining herself for the whole day there. Dwayne and I had to decide what to do about the growing fetus in my body, and to talk about what consequences our decision would have.

We had decided to meet at The White Horse - the start of

this whole thing. For some reason I was dragging my legs behind me after we landed. Our plane was delayed for almost 45 minutes, and I suggested that we would take the underground instead of a cab, but first I needed the restroom to freshen up, and then I convinced Sophie that we should have a quick coffee to calm my nerves. While in the underground we got lost and went the wrong way so we arrived to the pub almost 1,5 hour after schedule. I felt nervous about meeting Dwayne again. What would it be like?

And now we had this thing to solve. It was almost as I didn't want to meet him and have to make such a life changing choice.

"Where have you been?" Dwayne burst out when we walked into the pub. "I almost left?!"

It was long after lunch-time when we arrived, and The White Horse was completely empty on this Guy Fawkes Day, except for Dwayne standing in his white t-shirt by the bar. I walked straight into his arms and inhaled his scent. When he wrapped his arms around me and kissed me I felt completely at home and utterly ridiculous for having made us lose one of our important hours together.

"Eh, I think I'll get on my way lovebirds" Sophie said and walked towards the door. "I'll meet you at the airport check -in at eight, okay?"

I did a thumbs up, as I could't get myself to part my lips from Dwayne's to give her an answer.

"Come on, let's go" Dwayne mumbled after a while.

I just followed him to his car and not until we were in it I asked him where we were going.

"I have booked us into a hotel. My place is a dump in a shitty area, I don't want you to have to see it. And this is on the right side of town for the airport" he continued as he shot me a quick glance when I started to protest with a 'but I don't care about that', and then he fired away a smile. "It will give us more time together."

(W.h.a.t.a.l.o.v.e.s.t.r.u.c.k.f.o.o.l.I.w.a.s...)

I was convinced that he was taking me to a classy hotel and felt touched by the fact that he only wanted the best for me. I saw before me a big comfy bed, soft carpets and nice victorian chairs. A place worthy of taking a decision of life in. Therefor I got a bit surprised as we pulled up at the parking lot of a brown brick cubic building with dusty windows, out in the suburbs.

'Poor Dwayne' I thought. 'He really must stay in a shit-hole if this is better'.

We checked in, and I can only imagine what the porter was thinking when he realized that we weren't going to spend the night there. To rent by the hour can only mean one thing. And five hours must mean that someone is taking his - or her - time.

I had an unpleasant feeling when we entered the room. I realized that I didn't really know this man. And we had been surrounded by others and been under the influence of alcohol, music and laughter before we ended up alone together.

I put my bag on the floor and took off my jacket.

"So..?" I said and turned to him.

"Oh, come here baby."

He pulled me into his arms and we started to kiss. The boring surrounding was instantly forgotten and we fell down on the bed.

After hours of lovemaking and some dozing off in each others arms, kissing and cuddling, the time was rushing to its end. Dwayne put a hand on my tummy.

"Dwayne. We have to decide what to do."

"I know. God, it is so difficult. And hard to imagine. Are you sure that there is something in there?"

"Yes, Dwayne. I AM sure."

Then we used the rest of the valuable half-hour remaining of decision-time to make love again.

"What?! You two are hopeless!!" Sophie burst out when I met her at the airport again. "You still haven't decided what to do???"

She was in high spirit after spending all five hours at the Southern Cross chatting to the barmen, and telling each and every one trying to have a drink in there what our mission in London was and how this story began. She had even got them to sing-a-long in our old-time fashion and I felt a pang of a 'missing-out'-feeling. I felt uncomfortable to have to tell her that I hadn't been to his place but in a quite cheap hotel, and I had a long explanation on why that actually was much better than to be in his home (the start of many explanations in the future about odd things - why I hadn't met his parents, why he wasn't coming over, why....). I was happy that I had been in his arms but I felt that I had failed the mission.

"Let's not tell Mika that I am pregrant. We have to hide it somehow. It feels like Dwayne and I haven't come to a conclusion yet."

"I have made us sushi for dinner" Mika said the first evening as we were sitting in their spartanly furnished living room high up in a building complex in Singapore.
She and her husband had lived there for five months, and they had only got the most basic furniture in order for their two-year-stay. A big couch that looked small in the enormous stone floored living-room. A dark mahogany sofa-table, and dinner table and chairs in mahogany as well. Beds in the master bedroom and for my godchild Juliette, and a cot for their 6-months old Ted. Sophie and I were to share a big inflatable mattress in the spare room.
Mika had picked us up at the Changi Airport. Warm, humid air greeted us as we embraced each other in a longed for hug. All three of us had met the first year in the technical program in high school. Sophie and I didn't have much experience when it came to social life, men and partying - none in fact - but what we were lacking, Mika had. When we met she had brown eyes and wild brown hair which sometimes was colored in flaming red - getting the extra height by shaving foam, a punk rocker boyfriend reminding of Sid Vicious, she was dressed in punk - definitely never pink - and had a very sharp tongue which she used in various discussions involving human rights, feminism and democracy. She was going to be a journalist

but why she chose the technological program for that I never really understood. Probably to say fuck you to convention. Sophie's and my choice had been the more moderate 'it sounds interesting, and could be useful in the future' than 'FUCK YOU'.

Now Mika looked lovely as usual. Her wild hair was combed down in a sleek shiny page since many years, actually since she met her husband Ola six years ago, and her striped black-and-white pants, studded belts and army green jackets was replaced by navy-blue linen dresses and blouses, more suited for an expat wife and mother of two. She looked like a brunette version of Téa Léoni, except for a tiny gap between her two front teeth, which gave her a cheeky and perky, as well as sexy, look - the only telltale of her wild past.

"Eh - sushi" I said and gave Sophie a helpless glance. "Isn't that raw fish?"

"Yes? Don't you like it?"

"Actually - I'm pregnant."

"What?!!"

Mika turned around with an 'I-can't-believe-what-I- just-heard'-face. "You're pregnant? I didn't even know you had a boyfriend!" she continued and laughed. "My God - I'm in shock! You have to tell me ALL! What has been going on while I've been away?"

When we came back to Sweden after the ten days in Singapore I tried to get Dwayne to let me know what he wanted. One night I was determined to not put the phone down until we had decided what to do. But after an hour we still hadn't come any closer to a choice. Both of us were getting frustrated.

"Dwayne, I feel that I am in a part of my life that it is okay to have a baby. But I don't want to do something you're not okay with" I said finally.

He sighed.

"I've been all over the world Andrea, but there's no place I've ever wanted to be as much as I want to be in Stockholm right now."

My heart melted. I knew it was difficult for him.

"Dwayne, you are the one who has got experience of children. What is it like?"

"It is like having a little friend."

Now, that didn't sound that bad. To have a little friend by your side.

"Well I will have to contact the maternal health center anyway. I will do it tomorrow. And eventually I will have to tell my parents."

"Are you sure you want to tell them yet?"

"I have to. We are going to Australia in 6 weeks time, and independent of the outcome I have to tell them."

The next day I called a friend at work, Karen, that I had met through the Riding-club at work. We had never worked together but on one horse riding trip arranged by the club we had found each other in our mutual dry humor and preference of wild gallops in the woods, where the others preferred a more safe trot in the paddock. She had only a couple of days ago let me in on a secret. She and her husband-to-be had been on a wedding the first weekend in October and caught the love-bug in the air and she had gotten pregnant. The same weekend as Dwayne and I was reckless in bed. Now I had to call her and let her in on my secret as well but I got her to swear her silence since Dwayne and I hadn't decided what to do. I got the number of her midwife, who was conveniently situated a couple of blocks from work.

I felt paranoid as I went out in the park outside the office and took out the note where I had scribbled down the number. I didn't dare to call from one of the office phones since I feared it was bugged or that someone would sit in the next room and hear me. Although totally alone in the park, in the dark and cold month of November, I talked in codes.

"Hello, my name is Andrea and I am calling you because this is the place you should turn to when you are in a situation like me. But I am at work at present so maybe you know what I want without me telling?"

"Ah, okay. Are you pregnant Andrea?"

"Yes I am" I said and felt a rush of excitement.

"Then I shall book an appointment for you."

"Okay!"

"Is next week working for you? Thursday?"

"That will be perfect! Thank you!"

I felt all excited as I entered the office-building again, and walked straight into my old colleague and friend from my early days at the company, Annabel - actually a second

118

cousin to Mika (it is a small world) - and we had done some crazy things back in those days (gratefully before everyone's foolishnesses were spread via social medias). We had only worked together our first year at the big television company when I had chosen the path of studio productions and outside broadcast, and she went the more trendy way in trailer-production. Now she was married and had a two-year old son so we hadn't really seen much of each other since we were in different phases in life. I had told her about Dwayne though, on one of our rare lunches, and she was very envious of the tall, dark, muscular Londoner I had met. She herself was deadly tired of her own tall but skinny man who had all sorts of phobias, after living with him for years and now tried to raise a son with him.

"Hello bitch - long time no see!" we said almost simultaneously and gave each other a hug and a squeeze on the tits. We always had rough language, and strange rituals, between us.

"I saw you in the canteen the other day. Your tits look very pouty nowadays. I thought you looked pregnant" Annabel said with a loud voice.

I just roared out a real builders laugh 'WHOA-HA-HA', trying to sound like it was something utterly ridiculous and hoping it would masquerade the fact that it was true.

"Well your tits don't feel that small either - are YOU pregnant?" I answered and stared her intensely in the eyes to draw focus away from me.

"Actually I am" she answered with a smile and leant

forward "but it's a secret still. Just in the ninth week yet."
Nine weeks? That is about the same as me and Karen.
Jesus - Dwayne must have come to Stockholm in the fertility week of the millennium!

At the midwife I felt very welcome and special. I let her in on the fact that there was some difficulty in the circumstances between me and the father to be, and that we actually hadn't taken a decision yet on what to do. 'You will know what to do, just make sure that you yourself feel comfortable with the choice you make' was her answer.
She confirmed that I was in week nine, 7 after conceiving plus 2 for when I had my last period, and booked me in for a doctor's examination. Due date was estimated to my own birthday in the end of June, on Midsummers Day next year. I felt my brain twirl in my head.

Next step was to tell my parents. We had a trip to Australia booked, with a first stop in Thailand to celebrate New Years. My mother was turning 50 - my parents got me when they were very young, 18 and 21 - and I had decided to go with them. I might as well tell them now, even before we had made the choice. When I had found out that my unborn child's birthday had landed on my own birthday it felt like a sign. This was meant to be. And I realized that my parents must have made their firstborn in October too. But even if we didn't go through with it I needed to let them know. In that case I would probably be a wreck when going on the trip.

I called my father at work on a Friday afternoon and asked if I could come over for dinner the same evening. Then I asked if we could meet up at Brommaplan where my bus would come in, and if we could walk home together. We did that from time to time. From there it was a 45 minute stroll to my parents house and we always had things to talk about. In this case I felt that it was crucial that I could talk to my father alone first. He was always more sensible than my mother, and less judgmental.

After walking in the cold December-evening on the compact layer of snow, talking about work-related things for twenty minutes, I just spilled the beans.

"I'm pregnant."

"Oh. Damn" my father replied and then went silent.

"It is the guy I met in London this summer that came over here. He has been here a couple of times."

"I figured that."

"We are still talking about what we shall do. It is mad of course. But still - I feel like I am old enough to have a baby. And a part of me feels like: go for it. At least the baby will be made in an act of love."

"I see."

When we came home my mother met us in the hallway.

"What has happened?"

I wonder why we need a language at all between family members? They can always tell if something is going on.

"You better sit down" my father said.

Half an hour later, my brother walked in to join the Friday night family dinner. When he arrived the air was dense with tension, and he can pick up a vibe as a shark in the water.

"What's going on?"

"Well tell him Andrea" my mother said challengingly, still not able to get her head around the fact that her daughter, although 31 (and therefor 13 years older than when she herself had her talk with her parents - actually, I think it was my father that had to have the talk with them), was pregnant. Luckily my brother had inherited my fathers openminded view of life and just said 'oh, hmm, okay' and just wanted to hear more about this man that he never had met or yet even heard of.

The night before my doctor's appointment I went to dinner and bowling with my group at work, as an end-of-the-season thing. I was in a splendid mood, high on the fact that I had this big secret, and had to order my beer at the bar when no one else did since I had to hide the fact that it was alcohol-free. I called Dwayne between the dinner and the start of the bowling and suggested that we could let faith decide what to do since it seemed so hard for us to come to a conclusion.

"How about if I do a strike we keep it? Strike - in, no strike - you're out" I said all dizzy from the last months events, and the secret I had dancing around in my head together with the non-alcoholic beer.

"After all we've been through? It seems like a not so serious way to take such serious decision" Dwayne laughed. "Okay, sure - I will have my fingers crossed."

"Well I think it is as good as any. And I know you will keep your fingers crossed! Desperately." I said.

"You don't know what I'm hoping for do you?" he answered.

"Of course I do."

It would be unrealistic that he would hope for an outcome that would mean a child in another country, with a woman he had just met. I felt a ping of sadness.

"No you don't know, Andrea."

No, I actually didn't. And his answer didn't get me any wiser. But I felt I couldn't push it further since I actually was standing outside a rowdy bow ing hall.

"Well, I will know what you wished for if I do a strike or not. Your power over me is immense. I am going to the doctor's tomorrow, can we talk after?"

"I will call you tomorrow and we'll talk properly, okay?"

"Okay" I said and felt calmed.

I did four strikes in total that night.

* * * * * * * * * * * * * * * * * * * *

Saturday September 6th, 2014

The weekend arrives when I have decided to tell the boys. I had talked a couple of more times with Dwayne and said that I might come over to London with the boys at their October-break. I had been very specific about the fact that he and I had to talk before I would start sending them over on their own.

He still couldn't present me with a reasonable explanation about the situation. It was still 'it just happened'. And he couldn't actually understand how he could be involved in a thing like this. 'I think I am a nice guy, and I am always trying to do the right thing'. I am not sure who he is talking about. He hadn't done many right things in my book with his lying, cheating, refusing to stand up for his actions or taking responsibility for them, and his constant disappearing acts. When I reminded him that I had tried to break up with him twice during our years together, and asked why he hadn't made us go through with the split-up, he said 'I didn't think you wanted to'. His mind definitely didn't function as the rest of our's. 'I DIDN'T HAVE ALL THE FACTS DWAYNE!' The only thing that gives me satisfaction is when he tells me that someone has smashed the windows of his precious Cadillac Escalade one night. Maybe Gemma told her ball-chopping friend some of this story after all.

I ask him to make sure that he answers his phone on the Saturday that I have chosen, in case the boys want to speak to him after our conversation. We are going to our little summer cottage that I bought for us when the kids where small, in an allotment area, and I have prepared Jason with an enormous long explanation of why he has to walk the 5 kilometers from the terraced house that we're now living in (which we moved in to in 2005) and to the cottage with me, Alexander and our dog Cookie instead of taking the subway on his own. I feel that it is easier to talk when you are walking, and that your brain works better when you move. And there is a less chance of getting interrupted by a ping on the computer, the phone or a friend at the door. For once he doesn't argue about it, he seems fine leaving his computer games and have a walk in the sun with us. Maybe it can be too much gaming even for a fifteen-year-old? When I tell Alexander to get ready I get a response that I hadn't expected.

"Uncle Erik is picking me up. We are going to have a look at football shoes in some shops. He said he can drive me to the cottage afterwards."

Bloody kids growing up and making plans on their own! This is totally ruining my plans. I need to tell them on a Saturday so we'll be together the day after if we need to talk about it some more, instead of being preoccupied by school and work. I am not sure how they will take this. And I can't wait another weekend. Alexander has several football-games coming up and will be busy the coming weekend on a school trip, and I need to be able to involve more of my friends in this but I don't want to let everyone know before the boys. Jason comes downstairs and say that he is ready. How many more times will I be able to convince him to walk to the cottage with me?

"Okay, come on. Let's go" I say. I am a boss and a leader -
I am experienced in dealing with changed circumstances.
I decide to tell Jason first. It might be a good thing too. To
let them have a chance to melt this one by one instead of
getting disturbed by the other one's reactions.

As we have walked about 10 minutes of the one-hour-walk
I start to clear my throat. It is a beautiful sunny September
day as we pass some gardens with yellow and orange
blossoms: asters and enormous sunflowers, and pink,
white and lilac phlox which give the air a sweetened scent.

"I have something to tell you and Alexander. I will tell
Alexander when he comes back, but I will tell you now."

"Okay" Jason answers but shows no reaction what so ever.

"Daddy has done something bad to me, and I found out
about it a couple of weeks ago but I had to think things
through."

"Uhum."

"It has turned out that daddy was married to a second wife
when we met, and I didn't know about it. And now he is
together with yet another woman and he has been for a
very long time. For several years actually. And he is living
mostly with her in London."

"Well, that was somehow expected. Daddy is so good-
looking so it would be hard for him to be on his own."

"What??" I almost choke on my involuntarily laughter.
"What do you mean? Daddy can't be alone because he is
good-looking? What does that say about me? I can be
alone - am I not good-looking enough??!"

126

"But you have us mum. And I wouldn't know if you have had someone else as well" he fills in.

When did teenagers get so bloody clever? All this instant access to internet, tv-programs with Dr Phil and god-knows-what have made them more grown-up than grown-ups themselves.

"Well, I haven't been with anyone else" I say with a humpf. I feel like a teenager myself.

"I can understand that it can happen" Jason - Mr Smart-ass Teenager - continues. "If I liked one girl in one country and another one here I could see myself being together with both."

"Jason! You are supposed to learn something from this! This is NOT a way to behave. One have to make decisions in life, not just go along. One has to make sure that you don't hurt people along the way, and this is something that hurts. It always gets revealed at one point or the other. And the further it goes the worse it is! And even if it doesn't get revealed it is wrong!"

I am getting going know. Like if I can explain it clearly enough it will communicate via telepathy from Jason's brain to Dwayne's. After all - they are made of the same genes.

"I know mum, and I can understand that it is hurting you loads. But it doesn't affect me. As long as everything will be as normal as possible for me when I go to London, it will be alright. I love daddy anyway."

"Of course you love him, honey. And you shall continue loving him. I love him too but I hate what he has done, and

I can never forgive him for that. People can forgive most things, and one should be able to because we are not more than human Jason - we all make mistakes - but this is something out of the ordinary. Daddy has pushed this too far, and he should have, and could have, acted differently in the past."

"I know" he says.

We walk quietly for a bit. We have now passed the various gardens and are walking in a small wood. The scent of the pines is heavy.

"How are you feeling mum?" Jason finally says.

God, he is so grown up. I feel so proud that he is becoming a young man, a man who is concerned of his loved ones. Despite of his fucked-up father.

"I feel sad, and angry, but in the same time I can also understand how this could happen. I think it is wrong, but I can also realize that it comes to a point when it is difficult to tell. Especially when you are not used to take decisions and plan things like your father. I will survive this, and I will learn something from it. It feels better now that I've told you, and I will have to tell Alexander know. We will be fine".

"I'm going to punch him."

Now, Alexander has a different approach to the information about his father's secret life.

When Jason and I arrive at the cottage my youngest son comes running round the corner.

"Look, mummy! Cool shoes aren't they?"

"They are lovely darling. Can you come and sit here on the veranda with me and Jason for a moment please?"

He sits down in one of the black rattan armchairs without protest, and Jason sits down in the other. I look into his eyes and tell him the same thing as I told Jason.

"I wanna go to London now. I'm going to punch him in the stomach!"

I can see that his mind is spinning. He looks intensely at me.

"I hate him."

"No, Alexander, you don't. I don't hate him. I hate what he has done, but what he has done has been to me, and not to you boys."

He turns to Jason.

"What do you think?"

"He hasn't done anything to me. I love him. I'm not angry."

"Well I am angry" Alexander says resolutely.

Later in the afternoon, as I am standing outside doing the washing up, Alexander comes up beside me.

"Maybe you can meet a rich man now?"

"What? A rich man? Ha ha, why would I want to meet a rich man?"

"You have always liked Zlatan. Maybe you can try to get him?"

"But he has got a girlfriend and two kids already."

"That doesn't seem like a problem, does it" he says glumly.

I can't help myself and start laughing. Such wise and precocious kid already.

"Do you want me to meet someone else?"

"Yes" Alexander answers.

I ask his older brother the same question.

"Only if you want to" is Jason's response.

"Is there any chance of you and daddy getting together again?" my younger boy asks, "if he says he is really sorry?"

I have to explain to him as well why that is impossible, but I feel that it is a difficult balance act. Forgiveness is something we all have to be able to, and I don't want them to be brought up thinking that you can not forgive. I want them to feel that they can make mistakes in the future - and be forgiven by the ones that love them. But I don't want him to nourish any kind of hope that his mum and dad will come together again. Because that will not happen.

When we go to bed at night Alexander wants to sleep next to me. He puts his small arms around me and gives me a hug.

"I am on your side mummy."

In the morning I wake Alexander up with a kiss on his forehead. He is going to be picked up for an early morning game.

"Daddy is a dickhead" he says without opening his eyes.

"I know" I say and smile.

"I never want to meet that slut."

Oops, where did he get that term from?

"No Alexander, she is not a slut. She is a innocent as I am in all this. She didn't know about us. Daddy is a dickhead but she seems nice by the contact that I have had with her."

"I still don't want to meet her."

"Well, you don't have to now, but if she and daddy continues together you may want to meet her in the future."

"No. Never."

Stubborn little fellow.

FOURTEEN

Upside down you're turning me

At the doctors I found out that my uterus was the size of a fist, and the thing growing inside of it was about 6-7 centimeters and weighed about 20-25 grams. And that I had gained 2,5 KILOS. Now how was that possible? I felt very excited as I waited for Dwayne to call. I knew he was busy at work and I wanted him to be relaxed and calm when he called me. When it turned nine o'clock at night I was very irritated. I knew he sometimes worked late but wasn't he keen on hearing what the doctor had said? And if I did a strike or not? At ten I started to get angry and at eleven I was furious. How dared he standing me up at a moment like this? I refused to call him myself. 'I am a strong, independent woman, and he said he would call me - I am not a clingy broad that chases a man' I kept repeating to myself.

In the morning I called Sophie.

"It better have been something wrong with that f-cking phone-net in London because Dwayne didn't call me AT ALL last night, although he said we would talk!" I shouted very frustrated. "I am SO PISSED OFF with THAT man. I never want to have ANYTHING more to do with that Brando-lookalike. Why the FUCK shall you get mixed up with those BLOODY men for AT ALL?! I am going to stay single for the rest of my life! Alone-is-strong is going to be my signature!"

"Did you try to call him?" Sophie asked.

"Eh. No" I answered sheepishly.

"You should have called him."

With no phone call from him during the whole next day I decided to call him in the evening. 'I am a strong, independent woman, and if I want to talk to my man I call him - I am not a silly broad that sits at home waiting for a man or a call!'.

"Hi baby! What did the doctor say? Listen - this is my song to you" he said as he answered after the second signal sitting in his car. He turned up the music in the background and I could make out the words 'stay forever', 'my heart beating' and 'don't want to miss a thing'.

"Oh, Andrea - it brings out so many memories!"

"He is SOOO sweet!" I shouted when I called Sophie the next day. "He NEVER has to say a nice word to me again. He played a beautiful song by Aerosmith to me that I never heard before and I looked up the lyrics and it was SO ROMANTIC! And I have this little thing from him growing in my tummy. I'm starting to get maternity feelings about it - feels quite fantastic really!"

* *

Friday September 19th, 2014

In September it is time to do a long-awaited trip to the west-coast with the girls, my four best friends since my high-school days. We are going to borrow Jeanne's father-in-law's house in a small fishing village, and are all looking forward to lovely fresh seafood, wine and champagne and some talking-talking-talking. And maybe a bit of fresh air and walking as well. I meet up with Sophie, Katrina and Jeanne in the city centre after work, and we are going to pick Mika up, who nowadays lives in Gothenburg, on the way. I am so eager to share what has happened with them. And I feel very excited, like I'm sitting on some juicy gossip that I know will make their jaws drop when hearing it. Only it is not about someone else. It is about me.

After the first 4 hours drive to the second biggest town in Sweden (actually a five hour drive but Jeanne is a skilled driver and probably has been a Nascar-driver in her former life) we are able to pick Mika up early. We continue the last hour drive to the rugged coast and stop on the way to buy fresh langoustines, crabs, shrimp, sauces, avocados, crisps, nuts, salad, bread and cheese for at least a dozen people. As soon as we enter the house we shake up some Caipirinhas and start munching the snacks and chatting about everything and nothing. I look at my friends with warmth in my heart and feel so grateful and fortunate that I have such good friends. They have known me for a long time, from our crazy and insecure teens and through the experience of growing up. I am so relaxed with them. Neither of us have to put up a facade.

Mika has three children by now, another daughter that was born in Brussels where they went to live after Singapore, and is now going trough a divorce, on her initiative, after being fed up with the feeling of being in the company 'Family ltd' and now looked for passion rather than a partner in her life. We were shocked since the rest of us saw their marriage as THE perfect one and they had the role-model relationship we all thought we were looking for. She looked sparkling now that the ties of marriage were being dissolved.

Jeanne is as tall as me and has the same steady bone structure, green eyes and high cheekbones, but she is a brunette and has a bit more class about her. In our teens people often asked if we were siblings. She loves meeting up with friends and family, and always arranges big dinners and meet-ups. She loves to talk, talk, talk as well as walk, walk, walk. In the woods, out on the fields, in the parks. Appreciating the flowers, trees, grass and the sky.

Jeanne loves art and any kind of outdoor activities. Her dream when we were young had always been to have a big family, and long, chatty dinners with them, followed by evening walks on the countryside. She now has three children like Mika, and is living on the countryside, but had ditched the artistic, chatty boyfriend and married and gotten kids with a non-communicating man who read the paper at the dinner table and who's idea of outdoor activities is to chop wood. Alone. Her kids have inherited her husband's fondness for solitude. The dinners are eaten in haste, and afterwards the kids rush up to their rooms, getting stuck in front of various violent computer games, as they hate the outdoors. But Jeanne has solved the problem by getting a dog to pet and take her walks with. And have her long conversations to. Maybe you can't have it all with a man.

Katrina is blonde with sensual curves, and incredibly beautiful with striking eyes and lush lips, as well as goodhearted with a special soft spot for kids and animals. Her younger sister is strikingly beautiful as well, but tall and skinny, and works as a model in Barcelona. Katrina works within the church, without being religious, and takes care of refugees and unaccompanied children coming from countries in war, and had after several relationships with complicated, disturbed men finally found a nice, handsome man with a great sense of humor, who has his feet on the ground. They have two young children and also a dog. A stray, abandoned one of course, found in Spain. We admire Katrina's ability to always care for everyone else, and at the same time being strong and clever, she is not a push-over. She and her husband took over the title 'role-model-marriage and relationship' when Mika voluntarily stepped off the throne. Now when Sophie and Mika are divorcees, and I don't have my Dwayne, they seem like the only couple steady as a rock.

In the car I had told them the short version of the story: that I had found out that Dwayne has a girlfriend, that he had been married with another wife that I didn't know about when we had met, and that he had been living with that wife when we made the boys. The rest I was going to tell them after the dinner and champagne, as the late-night show.

After two bottles of champagne and in to our third, and after the delicious creamy pink and salty langoustines, the springy shrimps and meaty crabs, I reach for a spoon and formally tap on the glass.

"Okay girls, I think you are ready for the dessert. I have some emails that I want to read out to you, that will explain everything."

I'm enjoying this, feeling like the total drama queen. A shame it has actually happened. And happened to me. I clear my throat.

"Hi Andrea, I'm not sure if you know who I am - my name is Gemma and I am Dwayne's girlfriend."

My dear friends eyes get wider and wider as the story develops. When I read the angry and totally insensitive first emails from Dwayne's mother they shake their heads, like they can get around the fact that a man can be a total prick, but not the fact that his mother can respond with such 'blame yourself'-attitude and total lack of sympathy for the shock and turmoil the mother of her son's two children must have gone through, and lack of understanding that they had played a part in making his lies possible for such a long time. I read out the emails mechanically, as I by now almost know them by heart. It is only when I read the sentences about that Dwayne had pretended that Alexander didn't exist that I start to cry and have to take a pause from the reading since I can't see the letters due to the tears flooding.

My friends come around the table and give me a warming hug.

"This must have been awful for you, Andrea. And what horrible low life piece shit of a man" Katrina burst out, which is very strong words for her. "And his mother - how can she have let him go on?"

I feel the need of defending his parents, since it was only the first emails that oozed of insensitive goo, and after I had swallowed my pride and said sorry about my outburst, they had been really nice to me and understanding, and made excuses for their bastard son.

"They were probably in shock as well when they found out that this had come out. And getting accused of helping their son didn't probably hit home at that point. I think that they didn't know about Gemma for several years and by then the damage was already done. It wasn't their thing to tell."

"I can not understand how Dwayne can be apart from his boys so much, I have always wondered that" says Jeanne and shakes her head. Even though she sometimes complains about her husband he is always there for her and their kids. He wouldn't think of disappearing like Dwayne has done in the past, both when it came to our two boys and his firstborn Sebastian, when things got a bit rough.

As I am flicking through the emails from Gemma and Dwayne's mother, and have come halfway through the events of the August session, I suddenly see an email with **Gemma Littleton** in thick black letters. An unread email from her? How is that possible? I gasp as I realize.

"Girls. You won't believe this. Just as we are sitting here she has sent me a new one."

"What??!" my friends answer in unison.

"Hang on. I can't read it now. I will have to finish reading the previous ones to you first. I'll read it after. Shit. It really makes my heart beat faster."

To: Andrea Hunter 2014-09-19, 20:35
From: Gemma Littleton
Subject: (no subject)

Hi Andrea, it's me again.
You must dread reading an email from me - hopefully the contents of this one will be nicer than previous ones I have sent.

A hopeful thought just flashes up in my head before I can stop it: has she broken up with him??

I hope all is well with you. Dwayne tells me you are thinking of coming over with the boys in October.

My heart sinks down again. Still together. And they seem to have nice conversations about MY boys.

If the Swedish school holidays are the same as England I am assuming that it's the end of October. He said Jason is anxious about flying but Alexander wants to see him.
Dwayne has suggested that if you were willing to let Alexander fly over on his own they could stay here together in our house. Obviously I want to meet Alexander (that's if he wants to meet me) but I don't want to overwhelm him. I would imagine he just wants to be with his Dad. I wouldn't stay here as it might be a bit much for a first visit. I could stay with a friend to give them some time together.

Is that right that he called Dwayne a dickhead when you told him what was going on? If he did I like him before I've met him. You have obviously brought your sons up to be good judges of character!!!
Even if you do come over with one or both boys don't you think it would be good for them to stay here with Dwayne?
I totally understand if you are uncomfortable with the thought of the boys being introduced to me before I have met you so just let me know what you think.

Just to let you know the house is a smoke free zone so you won't have to worry about passive smoking like you do in Putney - I feel like I've been kippered when I come out of that house!!

Passive smoking suddenly seems less of a threat. It can't be that harmful for the boys to have a cloud of smoke around them while they eat, watch telly or sleep, can it?? Less worrying than a nice, beautiful, charming, easygoing, non-nagging new woman on the block around them.

If you do come over of course you are invited here - you must see where the boys will be staying in the future.

The future. Oh my god. Why can't she just disappear?

I am going to suggest to Dwayne that we visit Sweden - I have never been and from what I have seen it looks fantastic. We could come for a weekend and stay in a hotel. I would be quite happy wandering around on my own so Dwayne could spend time with the boys.
Dwayne doesn't know I have sent this email - I think he is uncomfortable with the fact we are in contact - maybe he thinks we will compare notes!!!

Hah. At least she keeps him in the dark about some things.

Get back to me with your thoughts,
Gemma

"What am I supposed to feel about this? How shall I respond?" I say helplessly to my friends.

"I think she sounds nice" says Katrina.

"I think she is a bit over the top" says Jeanne. "A bit hysterical trying to smooch things over, like she's really hiding her head in the sand."

Exactly my thoughts as well. How dare she pretend that it is only 'play forward' from now on? The kids just found out a couple of weeks ago, does she really think that this can be buried and forgotten, just like that?

"No, she's only trying to make it better, and tries to move forward from this horrible thing" Katrina insist.

"I don't like her. She sounds like a fool" Sophie - my blood sister, always on my side - interjects.

"Yeah, there must be something up-in-the-blue about her" Jeanne agrees.

"I can't understand any of this" Mika says. "I am probably still in shock. It sounds like something I would read in a book. And I still haven't met him. He's like Santa Claus, someone you've only heard of but never actually seen."

Katrina tries to develop what she means.

"Think about it, she must have been through hell as well. Imagine having lived with this man and found out about this. She is only trying to do the best in this situation."

"The best would be to run a hundred miles from him" I say bitterly. "She must be mad staying with him after all that he has done."

I still don't know how to respond to her email. I need to think about it and decide to wait until after the weekend, when I am at home again. I am grateful that my friends have different opinions and dare to say them out loud, I wouldn't want them to boost my ego and let me think that I am always right. But I can't help myself being a bit happy that Sophie and Jeanne seem to think that this Gemma is a bit... not right. In her previous emails it has sounded like she didn't tell the whole truth to her friends. Is that the reason she is able to make such a terribly wrong decision as to stay with him? Is she able to block out the warning signals because no one with a clear mind will talk some sense into her? Maybe she doesn't want to be talked out of it. Is she scared of being alone? Or to lose her status as someones girlfriend? Is she depending on his money to keep her lifestyle? Doesn't she have a drivers license and get nervous to not have access to Dwayne's driving skills and status car? Or is she just afraid to let people know she has been such a fool? I can really relate to the last thing.

FIFTEEN

Friday, bloody Friday

When one week of December had passed I was getting a bit desperate. I was now getting into my twelfth week and both Karen and Annabel had 'came out' at work and were sharing the news amongst their friends and family. I called Dwayne although I knew he was working.

"Hi, I can't really talk right now, I am really really busy. I need to work all night and I..."

"DWAYNE! For God's sake! I am in my third month! It has started to show!"

It hadn't actually, not to anyone else but me, but my belly was bound to pop out at any moment now.

"Okay. See you tomorrow."

I got confused and felt a rush of happiness. Was he getting over here? But then I heard a man that started protesting in the other end and felt guilty. I didn't know that he had someone in the car with him.

"OUT!"

I heard the door slam.

"Sorry Dwayne, I didn't know you had company."

"It's alright. He is a wanker anyway."

"Have you told anyone about this?"

"I've told Tom. He just laughed."

I felt comforted by the fact that he had finally told someone. Both for his sake, so he could get some form of mental - even if not moral - support, and also because it was making me nervous that he kept it to himself. Made me feel that he was trying to block it out or pretend that it wasn't real.

"What do you really think about me being pregnant? Tell me what you want. Shall we have a child together or not?"

Dwayne hesitated for a moment.

"A part of me is thinking it is fantastic, 'hell yes - let's go for it!' But the fact that we are in two different countries doesn't make it easy." (He could have added: 'and I am married and living with my wife'. That would definitely have added an extra dimension to the complications.)

"I know. If it was entirely up to me I will have the child, you know that. I am old enough, and I am ready to take my life to the next level. But I can't just decide to have this child, you are the father, it will affect you too."

"It will be harder for you than me. I am here in London so you will have to take the bigger part."

We sat in silence for a bit.

"Honey, whatever you wanna do I agree with you" he said

finally.

"Good. I have more or less decided that I want to keep it."

I could see him before me as I heard him draw a deep breath, and probably ran his fingers through his hair.

"I guess I will have to buy a plane then."

When we hung up I felt I needed to think about what he had just said. No talk about doing this together or of me moving to him in London, or him moving to me in Stockholm. For sure his 'buy a plane' meant that he had the intention of coming to Sweden more often, but not permanently live here. And I understood that he couldn't just leave his son in London behind. I had to decide this on my own. I thought about it the rest of the evening. About the feeling of having a life growing inside of me. That I have traveled - if not the world, then at least parts of it. That I am old enough. I'm in love with the father of the child and even if it doesn't last between us at least the child is made in an act of love (ehrm, well passion then...).

I am strong and secure enough to take care of a child on my own. Since he didn't say 'no - definitely not' I started to feel more and more excited and less focused on the problems involved. I felt very calm and serene when I eventually fell asleep, with the thought that if I continued to feel like this - then we have had a result, folks.

After our phone call that night my tummy popped out. It was like I had held my breath for the last couple of months and now got to exhale. I didn't tell anyone at work, I wasn't ready for that, but finally I was able to feel sheer joy about

the life growing inside of me. I had that walking-on-clouds
-feeling for two days and on the Friday morning I
discovered blood in my knickers.

It was just a little bit, and it was just a fragment of it when I
went to the toilet. I tried to relax. I knew that blood and
pregnancies didn't mix well, but it was just a tiny amount?
I called the hospital.

"It can sometimes come a little blood. Call us again if it
gets more than a couple of drops."

During the day at work I went to the restroom at least
every half hour to check. For every time with no blood in
sight I got my hopes up, and then there would be a third
visit to the loo with another couple of bright red
foreboding drops. I kept thinking about what could have
started it. I had continued my horseback riding lessons
every week but surely I had seen pregnant women on
horseback before? And I went to a hockey-game at the
Globe a week before, where my bottom had gotten chilled
- could that have had any effect? And the aerobics? I left
work early, blaming a headache, and went home. In the
afternoon it suddenly was like someone pulled a plug out
of me. Warm, dark red blood just splashed down in the
toilet. I panicked and called the hospital again.

"We can book an examination for you on Tuesday."

"Tuesday? But that is too far away? What shall I do in the
meantime? Is there something I can do to prevent more
blood?"

"If it is coming out, it is coming out. There is nothing you
can do to stop it if it is a miscarriage. It is just nature's way.

Come in if you get a temperature or cramps before Tuesday" said the practical and emotion lacking voice in the other end.

I called Dwayne. He seemed very worried about me, and I liked the protective sound in his voice. He asked me to take it easy, and said he wished he was there with me. I tried to hear if there was some hint of relief in his voice but I could only hear concern. And then I called my parents, and Sophie who immediately asked if I wanted her to come over. But I just wanted to crawl down in bed and to be alone. I wanted this horrible day to pass. No talk nor analyzing, or to think about it at all. All the weeks of thinking and talking back and forth about what to do, and now this new life, beginning to grow in my womb, was pouring out of me.

On the Saturday my parents and my grandmother and her sister came over to my place for dinner. I had planned to tell my grandmother about the good news but now it felt like it was a chance that it wouldn't be any news to tell. I didn't want to cancel the dinner because I was afraid that the time would tick in slow-motion, and when I woke up there hadn't come any more blood so I had decided to go on as planned. The usual lighthearted and chatty dinners with my granny was now a bit different though. Both my parents and I had our minds elsewhere and the worry laid like a blanket over the usually so easygoing conversations.

On the Sunday I went for my horseback riding lesson with the mantra 'if it is not meant to be there is nothing I can do to change it' but I skipped the gallop. And the trot. And then I rushed out to the toilet to have a check. No blood.

When the weekend had passed it was only Monday left before I could get the verdict. I met my father for a coffee and he tried to comfort me.

"There will be other chances."

"No. It won't."

Suddenly it felt that this had been my one chance in life to have a baby. To be a mother. Now that I had dwelled with all this 'am-I-ready-or-not' it felt like it would be impossible to plan for a thing like this in the future. With any man. It definitely wouldn't be any more chances with Dwayne. After this turmoil he would probably run a mile if I suggested we'd jump in the sack again, or wear triple condoms 24/7 just to be safe. He might never dare to see me again.

* * * * * * * * * * * * * * * * * *

To: Gemma Littleton 2014-09-23, 23:22
From: Andrea Hunter
Subject: Re:

Hi Gemma.

Sorry for the late reply - I've spent the weekend away with my friends (not many Dwayne-supporters there now...) and then I went straight to a two-day conference at work.
All your suggestions about London and Sweden visits sounds good. But I think it's too soon.

Both boys need to see their father, but they've said that they want everything to be as normal as it can for them. And if they come to London they need to spend time with their grandparents as well. I want the boys to ask about the new situation and be curious, instead of pushing new things on them.

I said to Dwayne that I will email you and let you know if I book a flight to London so that he knows that it's no point in keeping things in the dark. I have not booked anything yet though - you can be assured that I will let you know if I come over.

Right now I don't know what we will do though. I will talk to Dwayne to try to figure out what's best for the boys at this point and then let you now.

Take care!
Andrea

I still feel a bit confused. Is it something wrong with me? The friends that I have let in on this think I am acting so cool and too understanding, not being neither furious or devastated. Am I one of these super practical women with the feet steady on the ground, or...am I still in a state of shock? I arrange a meeting with another one of my friends, Maud. We go way back, and she has had her fair share of hard times in the past. When her husband decided that he wanted to try life as a gay man, she handled it pretty calmly. On the other hand she had been totally convinced that he would come back to her. They have always had fun together, and a great sex life. She thought that 'let the bird out of the cage' and all that. They had met when he was very young, and she figured that he needed to liberate himself a bit from the burdens of being a family man. The problem with letting the bird out though, is that there is always a chance that there is a bloody cat there to catch it. Of course her little birdie flew straight into the arms of a not-so-straight cat and - BAM - in the post arrived the divorce papers. Maud had been sad and shocked in the beginning of course. 'Now that our kids finally have left the home WE were supposed to do all these things we have kept on hold, like going away on love weekends, travel the world, run around naked at home!' Now that her ex-husband was doing all these things (only with someone else than her) she said she was happy for him. Bare in mind that it was four or five years ago now.

"I don't think you're crazy. You are just like me" Maud says as I fill her in on the details of Dwayne's actions, and my reactions.

We have the same humor so we both are laughing out loudly when I come to Gemma's description of 'rabbit-Dwayne', and both of us shake our heads and smile at the irony of how your life can take the odd turn. I think I prefer the odd turn of winning the multi-million lottery though.

"Both you and me know that it is never black or white, Andrea. There is no use in getting angry. Better to just make the best of it."

Well she certainly has. She had signed up for a dating-site - actually several ones - a couple of years ago, and now tells me vividly about all the different kinds of men she has met. All of them nice and fun. I wonder how she does it? In my eyes all men seem to be some kind of fifty-shades-of-a-jerk.

"I am having the time of my life, Andrea! You will have it too! It takes a while, but you just wait - when you are ready you will see how many nice men you still haven't met yet!"

Maud's eyes are twinkling and she looks very content and happy. I wonder when I will feel that. Will it take several years also? God! I am way too impatient for that. I decide to give it a year. One year tops! And THEN I'm going to start to live my life again.

I carefully listen to Maud's description of how it works out there in the dating-internet-space. She very generously offers to give me some of the men she has ongoing chats with, but I politely say thanks, but no thanks. At this moment anyway. It feels like such hard work. Keeping all those contacts on different sites going. How can you keep track of them?

Maud and I are having our drinks and dinner at Bistro Jarl close to Stureplan, sitting at one of the tables in their outdoor seating although it is almost October, facing the busy Birger Jarlsgatan. The French concept bistro was the first in Stockholm that had all their chairs facing the street, like in Paris, when it opened in the late 80's. A hangout especially attracting newly divorced men in their late 40's. This was their special afterwork-place and it was also a perfect place for single women to hunt, if you didn't want the competition of the young, full-lips, perky breast, younger women in tight pants that were hanging around the waterholes round Stureplan. Here the men were relaxed, chatty and out of the predator-mode which made it easy to land one. And it seems like a man have less problems going from one relationship to another. ('BUT WE WERE ON A BREAK!!' from Ross to Rachel in an episode of Friends echoes in my head). You had to be careful though, since the odd married man visited the place from time to time, wanting to hang out with his single happy-go-lucky friends. Now Maud has fallen for a man that was living in another city, and did a quick introduction of him as he stopped by on his motorbike to say hello to us, on his way to one of his meetings in the city. But just minutes before, we had been indoors to say hi to another one of her dates. I could never pull that one off. To me the dating business seemed like very hard work and not that appealing. But maybe later? (For those of you that want to rush instantly to Bistro Jarl now, to hunt a man on the rebound, I have to disappoint you. Although it did survive the decades round the millennium, it didn't survive the year of 2015. It just recently closed down. I don't know where the men have gone for their afterwork beer now. Probably to the English pub The Bull and Bear Inn across the street. Newly single men never go that far...).

SIXTEEN

"I love you"

The Tuesday came when it was time to do the ultrasound. Sophie was coming with me. We hardly spoke on the way to the hospital. I was comforted just by the fact that she was by my side, but I think we both knew that there was nothing we could talk about. We could not find out a subject that didn't involve what we were going to find out by the ultrasound, and to talk about what we might find out there was too hard. We sat in silence in the waiting room.

"Andrea Hunter?"

"That's me!" I heard myself say with a high pitch voice, and we were led into the examination room. Grey walls, white ceiling, sharp lighting. So it was here, in this sterile room, I was going to find out which way the future would lead me.

"Please take your trousers and knickers off and sit up in

that chair please" said the doctor and pointed at the direction of the gyn-chair. "We're doing an internal ultrasound to try to see what has been going on, okay?"

"Okay" I answered after having to c ear my throat to get the sound out. Sophie gave me a comforting 'it-is-going-to-be-alright' smile.

The doctor put the gel on what looked pretty much like a long, grey, very slim dildo. Sophie and I exchanged glances and in normal circumstances we would have burst out in laughter, but now we settled for lifted eyebrows.

The time between the dildo was in place and something comprehensive was visualized on the monitor felt like a lifetime. Suddenly she stopped her hand movements.

"Here it is. And the heart is beating.'

I gasped as I saw it. It looked like a tiny boxer with its small hands in front of a very big head. And a little dot in the middle of it was blinking. I screamed out loud and Sophie joined in as we had been on a rock concert seeing our big idol entering the stage instead of being in a hospital room. The doctor laughed at our monumental relief.

"But why did I bleed? What is going to happen? Is it going to stay in there?"

"I can see a small dark area at the end of the placenta. Probably a bit of that has come out. It can happen sometimes. Since it's just such a small area I think that was it and everything will be fine from now on. I can't promise anything of course, but it looks good from what I can see. You will get an appointment for a regular ultrasound check up at the end of January. Just enjoy the pregnancy."

There was no chance in hell that I wouldn't enjoy it from now on. I felt that the thorn-sprinkled rotten log that had fallen down and blocked the bright and sunny, blossom-decorated road that I had started walking on, suddenly had gotten vaporized, and now I could see the rosy road for miles ahead, drenched in sunshine.

I called my parents and they got relieved to hear the news. I didn't call Dwayne. I wanted him to show me that he was concerned and interested in knowing the result from the hospital-visit by calling me himself. He did.

"What's going on? Why haven't you called? What did they say?" he asked when he called a couple of hours later.

"We are going to have a baby" I answered with a calmness and a comfort that I hadn't felt in a long time.

"But why were you bleeding? Is everything alright?" he continued with worry in his voice.

I explained what the doctor had said, and he seemed pleased. We decided that he was going to come over to me when I came back from the trip to Australia at the end of January. It felt like ages but I knew that the three weeks 'down-under' would make the time fly.

To: Pete Roderick 99-01-25, 14:24
From: Andrea Hunter
Subject: G'DAY MATE!

Had a fantastic time in Australia!!!
Climbed Ayer's Rock, saw a shark while snorkeling, entered a

rainforest and enjoyed the warm, warm weather...!!
By the way - I'm pregnant! (=no more tequila...!!!).
My fantastic Englishman Dwayne and I are going to have a baby... Can hardly believe it myself but the rattling and kicking (very lively little thing in there - like me??!!) is absolutely real! I'm going to be a mother around midsummer (end of June)!!!!!! As you may understand it was not planned but now we find it very exciting! Can you babysit??!!
Lots of hugs 'n kisses!
Andrea

I was over the moon with love and excitement. I had talked to Dwayne a couple of times during the Australia-trip, but it had been difficult, not only by the time difference, but also for being out in the outback for several days at the time with no reception whatsoever. One night when I was sitting on the balcony at the hotel in Port Douglas, the phone rang. We had been out snorkeling all day, and I was sitting sipping an alcohol free beer while hearing the sounds of exotic birds in the treetops. We talked and talked, actually mostly me, about all the things I had experienced on the trip.

Then all of a sudden he said it.

"I love you, Andrea."

I was taken by surprise, that he actually said the words, and got nervous by the intensity in his voice and just laughed back. I wasn't sure he was serious, he was joking about so much.

"I know you freak out when I say this, but I do."

"Good!" was my reply, and after we hung up I banged the phone against my head. Why, why, why didn't I say 'I love you' back?! I had never said it to any man before. I loved my family and my friends, they were very close to me in my heart and in my mind, but I felt that I didn't really know him. I definitely was IN love with him. I was infatuated by him and his body. I longed for him and I wanted to be wrapped up in his arms. But I wasn't connected with his brain. I hadn't got a clue what he was thinking or feeling. About anything - not even me and the baby we were expecting. It was like his brain worked in a different language (which it was of course) but a language that I hadn't taken any lessons in. I felt that I had to use a dictionary every time he reacted and acted in ways I didn't expect, and had to add an equation as well to try to get the answer. I didn't have any key or code to his mind. Did he really love me? Was I in his brain? Did HE feel he knew me? Then I got mad with myself - he had his baby in my womb. Of course he loved me! God - poor thing. He must wonder why I didn't say 'I love you' back. Imagine the opposite! If I had said it to him and he would have answered 'good'. I would have gone over and over it a thousand times in my head and with my friends. 'What did he mean? What shall I do now? Shall I pretend I didn't say it??'. They would never hear the end of it. For Christ's sake, we were going to have a baby together! I decided that the next time I spoke to him I would start by saying 'I love you too', so it wouldn't be an issue.

"I love you too, Dwayne."

"Good" was his answer. Of course.

But from that day we kept saying it to each other. And the roller-coaster ride we had been on had miraculously joined the rails of the love tunnel with its smoother turns and less breathtaking surprises round the corners.

To: Andrea Hunter 99-01-26, 18:44
From: Pete Roderick
Subject: Re: G'DAY MATE!

CCOONNNGGGRRAAATTTSSS.

In fact, still in a state of shock of the news!! Gosh, how grown up. Looking forward to seeing you preggers!! Definitely will try to get to Stockholm in summer to see you (all!!). Maybe can coincide with Norwegies in Stockholm or Madrid - actually I suppose Madrid is now out, though maybe we should organize a swansong. Come to think of it, if you get over-due, dancing to Spanish music might help. In some ways it's a shame we never had a son - now THAT would have been one Crazy Carrot!!

Glad to see Dad is from a proper country, not a minority one like Scotland. Are you going to live together? I suppose the same countries would be a start.

As you will probably gather I am shooting in all directs at the moment, so will have to rush off.

However, wanted to send greeting.

Best wishes and lots of besos.

TheOriginalCrazyCarrot.

When I got back to Sweden I couldn't stop saying 'I love you' to Dwayne when I spoke to him. And he seemed thrilled that I was back on Swedish ground. Finally we could have our evening chats without worrying about astronomical phone bills, and bad reception. He had booked a flight for the first weekend I was back. I had been on the planned ultrasound, everything looked fine, and I had gotten a printed picture of our child and I was eager to show it to him. And I wanted him to meet my parents. After spending every day with them for three weeks on the trip it felt strange that they hadn't met the father of their firstborn grandchild. But when he arrived the temperature dropped to a freezing minus 18 degrees and he convinced me that we should stay in bed in each others arms so we hardly got out of it, let alone the flat. He told me he was on medication due to high blood pressure and had a mild heart attack at the age of 30. He had gotten off a plane with a pain in his arm, and when he saw the doctor the examination showed that he had a minor heart failure. It didn't sound that dramatic when he told me about it and he assured me he was strong as an ox. I thought he was lucky to have met me, since I wasn't the hysterical type, and was low-maintenance. I wasn't the type of girl that would put any pressure on him.

* * * * * * * * * * * * * * * * * * * *

October, 2014

In October my anger starts to build up. I have started to get extremely irritated over Gemma's email in September, and I am not at all interested in making it easy for Dwayne by coming over to London with the boys. Even Jason says 'let him come over now, we have been over enough, he should make the effort'. Yes! Exactly! HE should make the effort to see his boys and talk things through with me.

Eventually I feel strong enough to let some of my other friends in on what has happened since I saw them last. I met Celia when Jason started nursery, when he almost immediately started playing with her second son. They were so small and cute when they started doing things together and you could actually see some kind of bond forming between them. Celia is my total contrast. Pregnant with her third child when we met, married to her high school sweetheart, working as a PE teacher and extremely energetic - drove her kids to nursery, then lifted out a bike from the trunk and went off cycling 10k to work. They are always inviting people over for casual dinners, and she is easygoing, openhearted and openminded, and every free second is spent on the go. When I feel that my weekend is fully booked after having one thing planned on the Saturday OR the Sunday, she can go from lunch at her mothers, having coffee with one group of friends and then going to dinner with some other acquaintances, and in between that watching one of her sons playing a soccer game, and then going shopping with their daughter. And that is just the events on ONE of the weekend days. I am a bit envious of everything they manage to do together, and I blame it on the fact that I am living as a single mother - imagine what you would have the energy for if you were two grown ups in a family! But I also know it is most probably because I have a bit more introvert personality. I charge my batteries when alone, and need my own space and time to reflect, but on the other hand when I finally meet people I behave as I am a full blooded extrovert person. Celia is the one and only of my friends, actually the only one I know at all, that has done an Ironman. She had connected with Louise a couple of years before I met her, when Celia's oldest and Louise's youngest son had became friends at the nursery. We all had such a nice time during the nursery years, and thanks to them I wasn't isolated, and was invited to dinners, playground picnics and trips.

Louise, Celia and Celia's old time friend from high school, Marilee, decide to meet up at the Lydmar Hotel one October evening after work. They have a cool lounge perfect for chatting. We haven't met for several months and they don't know what has happened. They had only met Dwayne once, but they had met him at least, when Celia and her family had a 'finishing-the-drink-cabinet' before a five year stay in the US. Probably thought he was kind of boring. An Englishman who didn't drink beer or whiskey, and was eager to leave early.

"What an asshole. Men! What idiots! I can't understand why they are behaving like pricks!"

Louise arrived early and is sitting outside the bar in the light of the descending October sun, and I can't help myself giving her the short version of the story before the others arrive. She is beautiful. A slim, single mother of two almost grown up sons, with a history as an air hostess, and a fair share of lying, unfaithful men. She could give me the fuel I needed for the bonfire of rage that I had started to create after having spent the first two months being fairly understanding about why this had happened. We indulge in prick-like behavior of men we know or have heard of by our friends and come to the conclusion that the only decent man we have in our close environment is Celia's husband, who is with her through thick and thin. Even if he is not great when it comes to talking about feelings, more the practical type, but at least he is there. When Celia and Marilee arrive I do the long version but they seem moderately surprised. I guess they have also heard a lot about bastard-like behavior when it comes to men. During our drink session it turns out that we all have problems but of different kinds. Worrying about teenagers going through difficult stages, different work related problems and Celia is also on the verge of a burn out-syndrome. It feels kind of comforting knowing that I am not the only one lacking a smooth life but at the same time depressing. What happened with all those happy-go-lucky days? Do we have to wait until we reach 'the second spring'? Being grandparents and having a pension? Seems like a long wait. On the other hand - time flies scarily quickly nowadays...

I have yet another long conversation with Dwayne trying to understand how this could happen and how he was able to face up to both of us.

"But you are living with her Dwayne, how could you face her after spending days and nights with me and the boys?"

"I'm not exactly living with her, I've always had my own place."

"Spending all your time with her except for one night a week at your parents I don't exactly call 'having your own place' Dwayne", but as I say it I think that it is probably how it is in his own head. He has always had problems with time. When I had reminded him that it has now been 3 months since you saw your sons he always replied 'is that so? Time goes so quickly don't you think?' and I would always - always - reply sourly that 'no, I don't think it passes quickly, I think it feels like ages since we met, and imagine how it feels for the boys!'. Probably living two (or more lives) have the time-speeding-effect on you.

"How could your parents go through with this? How could they face both me and her?"

"She haven't met them that often."

"But why not? Wouldn't she want to be more with them, didn't she wonder why you didn't spend more time with them?"

"No, I don't think so. Gemma is a very solitary person. Her mother died very young, and she fell out with her father and didn't speak to him for years. She has broken it off with her brother."

I shiver as I hear him say her name. 'Solitary person'. Is that

164

why she has to cling on to Dwayne? Because she hasn't got any close friends and family? Maybe she hasn't nurtured her other relationships during the years with Dwayne. If she is so alone maybe I should feel sorry for her. But I don't. I think that she must have made loads of wrong decisions over the years and is herself to blame for them.

"Well I'm lucky to be single now, instead of stuck in a sour relationship like you. Eventually she will wake up and realize what a prick you are, or she will be so suspicious of you that she eventually will drive you mad. Your relationship is doomed, Dwayne."

To: Gemma Littleton 2014-10-24, 07:29
From: Andrea Hunter
Subject: Status update from Stockholm

Hi Gemma.

Here comes a status update from what's going on here:
The boys need to see their father, and I need to get closure on a 16 year relationship.

1,5 months ago the boys thought their mum and dad loved each other. Now they know we're not together any more. And above that, their dad has been involved with someone else the whole time.
Jason is fine with it he says, as long as it doesn't affect him and that he doesn't have to see you. He wants to be with his dad, and meet Sebastian, and when he is in London to stay with grandma

& grandpa and that his dad is going to be there. This is what he said when he found out and this is how he still feels.

Alexander - who is younger - is very angry. With Dwayne, and with you. But he loves his dad of course. But he is very affected by the fact that you exist, and he has called you loads of things and he hates you. I have every time this comes up said that Gemma didn't know and it is not her fault, but he still says "I don't even want that girl to come over the Swedish border". It is not easy for him to grasp this.

Dwayne knows that this is the boys reactions and feelings. He also knows that I need to sit down and talk to him so we can end this relationship in a proper way. I need closure, and after 16 years I think I deserve that. Not just to get the information in an email from his current girlfriend. I have also told him that I will contact you with anything involving him and me meeting, so he knows I will tell you if I come over to London or if he comes over here.

At this point I think he should come over to Stockholm to show the boys he makes the effort and that he wants to see them. And to make less hassle for me. He needs to give them his undivided attention when he is here, and be here when they go to sleep and when they wake up - as usual. He or I can stay on the couch, or I can stay at my parents or at my friends - depending on how much we are able to talk things through. And I will need to talk to him to be able to move on. At least you have had that opportunity.

As I said before - I have no interest in him as a man anymore. Even though I am a very understanding person, and can forgive most things because I know we are not more than humans, but a man that can act like this and has behaved the way he has for so long, *is not someone to be in a relationship with. And he will keep withholding truths, because he is not able to make decisions and stand up for what he thinks is right if it means someone is getting hurt or angry. That makes him feel unpleasant and for some reason he can't take that. Upbringing? Rejection? Borderline personality? Other damages? Whatever it is I don't care - he doesn't seem to want to work on it or figure it out himself and then it is hopeless. He acts exactly like an alcoholic, with the lies, broken promises, deceiving etc, but instead of drowning unpleasant feelings in alcohol, he drowns them in lies, trying to keep everyone happy so he doesn't have to have anyone have a go at him. The result is totally the opposite though...*

If you and Dwayne still are together a couple of years down the line then of course you will see the boys and be involved in that part of Dwayne's life (I think that is what you want - I would have wanted that after being kept in the dark for so long). The boys will probably be calmer about this, and grow an interest in meeting you, when they feel that you haven't stood in the way of meeting their father even after this came out.

Take care.
Andrea

SEVENTEEN

"He has got kind eyes"

"Oh, yes, Elvis" said my mother and pulled out an old LP-record from the shelf and pointed at the all-in-white and eagle-decorated world-wide famous singer. I wanted to sink down through the floor. Jeez, we all sounded retarded in the family. My parents, who usually were quite good at both understanding and talking the well known language, now sounded like the typical comedy movie characters 'Inga and Sven from Sweden' and had started using sign language instead of talking. And Dwayne was sweating floods while trying to hold the small white-and-gold cup of coffee with his big hands. I regretted that I had insisted on the 'meet-the-parents'.

It was April and Dwayne had come over again. Three months seemed like an eternity but when we met it was like we had never been apart. And during that time I had gone flat-hunting so I had been pretty pre-occupied. After a couple of lost bid-sessions I had finally gotten my hands on a big two-room apartment that would be perfect for me and a child, in Bromma. Easy to reach for my parents on their way home from work, and I was going to be able to move in about three weeks before due-date. That a child could decide to arrive early wasn't in my head at all. I was in charge of the planning. (So I got pretty shocked when Karen called and asked me to come to the hospital with her since she was in labour while the father-to-be was on his way home from a business trip. He arrived on time to see their baby son born nearly seven weeks early. Maybe everything wasn't plannable?).

I knew I was dependent on my parents to get things to work with a little baby without Dwayne around, but the flat was big enough to fit him also if he decided to move over. I wanted him to feel welcome if he decided to take the step, but I didn't want to force him. My philosophy had always been that you have to be in charge of your own life to feel good about yourself and to be able to be a good partner, and no relationship benefits from constraint. (Now I am not so sure anymore. A mild push over the obstacle spelled w-i-f-e, might have been useful in this case...but I DIDN'T KNOW ABOUT HER DID I?!).

I had by now gotten some more pieces about his life. He was kicked out from his parents house when he was 16, and had worked ever since. Apparently his mother got fed up with him and the trouble he was causing. He also hadn't seen his parents for the last couple of years after a fall-out so they didn't know he was about to be a father again. He said he really didn't want to have anything to do with them any more. I thought it was strange, don't you try to make up when you fall out? But I thought that his reluctance to talk about it was due to the fact that it probably was very painful for him. He had agreed to meet my parents on this trip though, and I was both nervous and excited about it.

I met him at the bus terminal, all calm and serene. I was wearing a striped blue and red tight t-shirt that accentuated my belly, which had now become quite big. When he saw me he pulled a scared face.

"My God! Look at that! What has happened?"

I was very pleased. I knew I looked fantastic. My skin was glowing, I still looked fit and the only thing sticking out was my belly and my breasts had lifted to new levels. The hormones rushing around in my body almost made me explode of happiness when I saw him. He was going to stay four days this time and the third day was planned for him to meet my parents.

On the morning of the third day I decided that we had to get out to let some fresh air in to our love-bubble. We left my tiny flat in the 5-level high old building in Råsunda, a municipality in the outskirts of Stockholm, and walked down the street in the bright spring sun. From the different pastel colors apartment complexes in the more city-like area we entered an area with villas, and the further away you got from my flat the bigger the villas. White concrete ones mainly, with big windows, pillars and glass-surrounded balconies, and then the odd green or pale yellow wooden cube. I secretly wondered if we were going to move into a house together some day, and live like a family. It sounded like he hadn't much strings attached to London family-wise. Except for his son of course. I knew he couldn't just leave him behind. Where the villas ended a lake and bird sanctuary started, named Råsta-lake. Thousand and thousands of birds tjirping, quacking and screaming. Seagulls, ducks, geese - you name it - every bird was to be found there.

"Can't we just go back to bed after? Do we have to go to your parents?"

"Dwayne! Of course you have to meet them! And they need to meet you. You are the father of their first grandchild!"

"But I'm not really good at that kind of thing. It is so nice to just stay in bed with you. I can meet them next time" he continued hopefully with a pleading look.

I felt disappointed. I didn't want to force him but still I wanted to share him with my family. And I didn't like that he was trying to keep out of the radar.

The lake was quite long but not that wide and as we slowly strolled the pathway that surrounded the shimmering water, my hand in Dwayne's, I started to feel like a goose myself. Not because of me quacking - we couldn't really talk because of the deafening noise from the birds - but because of my duck-like walk. The belly kept pressing down on my bladder and I didn't want to risk peeing in my pants when walking with the man of my dreams, who was also going to be the father of my firstborn child. The other birds around us didn't mind holding their bits though, and from out of nowhere came a big white splash that landed straight on one of Dwayne's shoulders. I almost wet myself then with laughter. (Seems like at least one of the Swedish birds spotted the fake bastard already then...). Eventually I got him to agree on going home to my parents for a quick coffee in the afternoon.

After a first extremely awkward half hour my father asked if Dwayne wanted a whiskey. I knew that he didn't like it, and shouldn't drink it due to his heart condition, but to my surprise he said yes. I felt so sorry for him. He must be extremely stressed out about the situation. Not until we sat there I started thinking about what it must be like to meet the parents of a girl that you had knocked up the third time you had met her. But miraculously the whiskey loosened the tongues of both my parents, and Dwayne seemed to relax and started to show his charming personality, so when it was time for us to leave we were all in high spirits. My father hugged me and said 'he has got kind eyes' and I knew that he had seen what I had seen. An honest and decent, as well as a charming, good-looking, hardworking man.

* * * * * * * * * * * * * * * * * *

Memories, from the corner of my...

kitchen

On the verge of entering the long, dark, wet month of November, I need to close down the little summer cottage for the season, before (hopefully) the snow lays a protecting blanket over the garden.

When I enter the abandoned house, that now has a gloomy, moist touch in contrast to the warm embrace I always feel there in the summer, my eyes spot a note that I have saved from years ago. It is attached to the door of the fridge, held in place by a magnet from the EuroDisney-trip the boys and I took with Dwayne and Sebastian. We are all sitting in the car of a roller-coaster type of thing and we are screaming with laughter. Except for Dwayne. He has put the jacket over his head. I was so mad with him when I saw the photo. It was a great family picture - or rather - it COULD have been a great family picture, if only he had shown his face. Dwayne was just laughing. 'I thought it was going to splash water!'. In hindsight it looks like he didn't want to be seen. The note behind it is a lot nicer. It is from when Dwayne was here for a month round my 40th birthday. In 2007. He had been dating Gemma for five years then. But he wasn't living with her. We kept writing little notes to each other every time we passed the notepad in the little kitchen. On one bit he had written 'Presence strengthens - absence sharpens' and a big heart. It was after we had laid in each others arms and talked (or was it only me?) about how difficult it was to be apart, but that it sometimes wasn't only bad. I tried to explain to him that I wanted us to be together more often, but that I was rather content living apart, and from watching my parents and my friends I knew that everyday life together wasn't always like a bed of roses. That I could do well without the everyday nagging about doing more (or less) cleaning, who's time it is to pick the boys up, and the 'do you REALLY have to watch the football AGAIN?!!' I got so happy when I saw what he had written, and wrote back 'Ah! You're a poet my fantastic man! I LOVE YOU!'

Now I get the urge to google the phrase. Maybe he didn't make it up after all.

Of course not. Turns out to be a quote by Thomas Fuller. Also used by Benjamin Franklin. When I search I can see that someone has asked the innocent question: 'What does this mean? Absence sharpens love, presence strengthens it?'. Someone has answered: 'There is a saying that absence makes the heart grow fonder. But there is also: Out of sight - out of mind'. Hah. A kindred spirit. I definitely know what that one is talking about. That's what it must have been like for Dwayne. I thought we were living apart by choice, instead it was because he didn't want to make a choice. Bastard.

In the evening, when I'm back at the house, I get a reply from Gemma.

To: Andrea Hunter 2014-10-26, 19:45
From: Gemma Littleton
Subject: Re: Status update from Stockholm

Hi Andrea.

Had to think things over before I replied to your email so apologies for late reply.
I have spoken to Dwayne about going to Sweden and him staying with the boys at your home. He does not want to do this as he feels it would be inappropriate given the situation.

HE thinks it is 'inappropriate given the situation'? Yeah - sure. More like SHE thinks. And why isn't he the one telling me this?

I think it is a reasonable compromise that I go with him and keep out of the way so he can give the boys his undivided attention.

'Reasonable compromise'. Hah - more like 'I don't dare to let him out of my sight'. Maybe she has googled and found 'out of sight, out of mind' too? What does she think he will do? Elope from her and stay with us? Well - it would actually be a thing Dwayne could do. Just leave and never go back. And not get in touch either. Too uncomfortable to hear someone get upset. But for him to be able to do that it would mean that I would take him back. Surely she can't think that? What woman would take back a man like that? Oh yeah - Gemma did.

175

I have to rephrase: what smart woman in her right mind would do that? That is right - no one.

I am sorry they feel the way they do about me but I think it is a normal reaction and I am sure as they get older it will be easier for them to accept me. Anyway - this is not about me. It is about Dwayne keeping in contact with his sons. We all have to accept that things will never be as they were.

Eh - I know that. I have never expected that. But going from a long term long-distance relationship with a man I love, and who is the father of my children, to: 'here-is-daddy's-new-long-term-girlfriend, let's be happy-go-lucky -from-now-on' is a bit too big a step. Let me and Dwayne break up first, I think as I realize that we actually haven't broken up. Even if it is quite obvious that we are not together any more.

I know you want things to stay as normal as possible but unfortunately that can not happen. It's not fair but life isn't fair is it, especially when Dwayne is involved.
As for you getting closure - Dwayne does not do closure, he walks away - always has and always will.

Hm. That sounds interesting. Sounds like she is talking out of experience. Has he done a walk-away from her as well? Was that in 2007 maybe? It might even have happened more times?

Your comparison of Dwayne and an alcoholic is very accurate. If you look at this situation like that, at the moment he is in rehab - detoxifying himself of lies. He is showing me texts you have sent to prove he is not keeping anything from me. Let's hope he makes a successful recovery!!!!

Ha ha - I knew it! Dwayne is so secretive about everything so she will probably feel very secure with him doing this. Maybe she haven't even asked to see them. If she has he will hate it. And if she hasn't and he is doing it anyway it is just one of his charades to keep her calm. He probably erases texts that he doesn't think is 'appropriate'. This relationship can't last for long. Either she wakes up to her senses, or he will get tired of her nosiness and distrust.

You are right when you say he does not want to hurt anyone but unfortunately it is inevitable that will happen.
Dwayne thinks it would be best for the boys to come over here - at least if they stayed at their grandparents that would feel somewhat normal for them.

I have told Dwayne that he really needs to "man up" and be honest. There is no point in him telling me one thing and telling you something different.

Please let's keep everything civil - there has been enough upset already.
Take care,
Gemma

To: Gemma Littleton 2014-10-26, 23:34
From: Andrea Hunter
Subject: Re: Re: Status update from Stockholm

Hi Gemma!
I didn't really expect an answer from you but I am glad you answered so thank you. I might answer a bit too quickly, especially since I had wine to dinner, but here it comes anyway!

Well - Dwayne can't walk away from this one, not if he wants to see his sons. I need to speak to him face to face - in London or here. And I'm sorry but I don't think it has been enough upset - maybe you feel that because you've been there and had a chance to deal with it, but I haven't and that is yet to come.
I'm glad that you can see the similarity with an alcoholic. Some of the steps to recover is:
- *making amends for past errors*
- *learning to live a new life with a new code of behavior*

Right now I can't see that the rehab is working. He still can't admit that you are living together. And trusting him because he shows texts seems a bit naive. It is very easy to delete texts that isn't showing 'the right thing'. Now I understand his strange polite 'thank-you' texts that always comes like out of the blue and doesn't connect with what we talk about. No wonder he refused to answer my last text and called me instead.

I want her to get a bit insecure with the notion of us talking to each other.

*You and I have one goal in common - that Dwayne will "man up",
but I don't think neither you or I would consider it manly to be a
marionette - acting after a script that you or I have written. And
he will never 'recover' as long as everyone else around him protects
him from bad feelings, and makes decisions and handles things for
him. Around alcoholics there are always co-dependent loved ones
- making the drinking (lies in Dwayne's case) possible.
I'm looking forward to hear what Dwayne has to say after this
weekend - hopefully something with his own words.
Take care,
Andrea*

A couple of days later I speak to Dwayne in the morning on
my way to work. He seems angry and irritated when I ask
him when he is planning to come over.

"I'm coming in November, and Gemma is coming with me,
enough said."

"Why does she need to come? This is about you seeing the
boys, and you and I to talk things through."

"You have made it very hard Andrea, since you've been in
contact with Gemma. She has to come with me, she wants
to be with me."

I feel content when I realize that my email must have
made a big stir in their everyday life. Hopefully she had
been mad with him and made his life hell for at least a
couple of days.

"Fine" I say, being happy that I am not with a man who
can't say that HE wants me to come along.

November, 2014

I November I start to feel calmer. The thing that upset me most - the fact that he didn't tell Gemma that Alexander existed - doesn't hurt any more. I realize that in Dwayne's life, and for everyone else in his life - his friends, family and relatives, he existed big time. It was only in Gemma's life he wasn't a part, and that I had no problem with. It felt that it was worse for her to not be let in on Dwayne's full life, than it was for Alexander himself. And I did understand that when he started dating Gemma, it would have been impossible for him to tell. How could he be open about having a 7-month pregnant girlfriend when jumping into bed with her?

I also have a couple of late night conversations with Dwayne. Again he is so sorry for what he has done. I am very determined that we shall have our 'closure'-talk face-to-face (in IRL I add - not Skype), even though he can't understand what we shall talk about.

"I just need you to face me Dwayne, and say that you are sorry. I don't want a different outcome, I just need to have a talk with you so I can move on. Don't you think I deserve at least a couple of hours of your time, after all these years?"

"You deserve a lot more than that Andrea. A lot more."

Funny then that November comes and goes without him coming over. Neither with or without Gemma.

EIGHTEEN

Preparing for the future

The first weekend of June it was time for me to move to the new flat.

I felt very grown up when I went to IKEA and bought a proper dinner table with four chairs, a king size double-bed and a big couch with a matching armchair. At the old second-hand rented flat I had used a fold-up garden table and chairs, a second-hand bed and a couch that I found abandoned in a basement that I just threw a pink quilt over to cover the old stains. (I now wonder how the flat or house looked like, that Dwayne lived in with his second wife. He must have felt that he was in a dump when he came to me in Stockholm. No wonder he just wanted to stay in bed all day). The new flat felt enormous since it was almost twice the size of my Råsunda-flat, and I thought that I had been very clever to have chosen one just a half-

181

floor up, and with a balcony, so I could both get fresh air when the baby was asleep as well as easily get the pram up in the flat. My friends had donated their old pram and a baby-cot so when I for the first time went to Baby World I only had to get a babysitter and a nursing table. I didn't dare to buy any more baby-clothes, even if I was in charge of the planning. It seemed like challenging fate. On Dwayne's April-visit we had gone in to the city and at the most expensive department store in town, the NK, we had together chosen a little short sleeved baby-body with light blue shells on it (Dwayne was quite certain by that time that we were expecting a boy), a white baby hat and tiny tiny white socks. I wanted that to be the first clothes our baby would wear. It felt like a very important moment choosing our first unborn child's clothes together. I was also very pleased with my big bed. Everything was ready for both arrival of baby and man (but it turned out that delivering a baby to the flat was a lot easier than delivering a man to it...).

* * * * * * * * * * * * * * * * * * * *

December, 2014

In the middle of December the draw for the round of 16 in the Champions League is finished. Zlatan and his PSG is meeting Chelsea at Stamford Bridge in March. I keep wondering what to surprise Alexander with this spring when he turns thirteen and THIS would be the perfect thing. And if Dwayne would take him that would probably break the ice between them - Alexander would never hold a grudge against him if he had a chance to see Chelsea live. But for that to come real Dwayne would have to come over first. I would never send Alexander to London on his own unless Dwayne and I have had 'our talk' first. I haven't been in contact with Dwayne since late November. I suddenly think that I shouldn't think so much so I just send him a text.

Get tickets for Chelsea-PSG in London for Alexander.

Straight away I get an answer.

And for J

Why would he get tickets for Jason? He is not into football at all, and it isn't a very wild guess to think that the tickets will cost a lot. Why get it for someone who doesn't appreciate it?

What do you mean? I answer back.

Jason as well he answers.

God - he is so thick. Of course I understood THAT. I don't answer him. Well aware that he won't get any tickets unless more spoken of. But at least I thought about it. I can always say in the future that 'mummy thought of it but your useless father never got it to happen'.

A couple of days later I get another text from him.

Hi hope you're well I have put money in to your account today some money from my parents for christmas and I am sending presents in the post and cards from me so you can put the rest of money in them from me thank you

How about seeing your sons? In a couple of weeks it will be one year ago is my pungent reply.

This is crazy. How can he be able to not take action to see his sons? He hasn't seen them for almost a year. Surely he can not be THAT afraid of me? Or is it Gemma who is keeping him in a tight grip?

I will be coming over in jan I've sent parcel with cards could you please put money in them thank you

So it is January now. What ever happened to November and December? And these 'thank-you's' are really getting on my nerves. But on the other hand it feels good that we can have a communication. And the money is always welcome.

For some reason it feels like January is really going to happen. I have been fooled before but no one - not even a psychopath dick - would be able to stay away from his lovely sons for more than a year?

Two days before Christmas whi e I am sitting on the subway on my way to work I read a new text from him, from the night before. I feel quite content about everything right now. The wounds are slowly starting to heal, I feel sure that he will finally meet his boys soon, and that I will have a proper talk with him. I don't want to change the outcome - I just want to get closure. I desperately need it to be able to move on.

Evening hope your well has the parcel arrived on the tracker it has I sent money did you get it

Oh how funny his texts are. I always have to read them several times to get the meaning of them, without the punctuations it can always be misunderstandings. I feel in a very happy mode when I answer him.

Arrived! I have put the money in the cards, boys will open it on xmas eve. I won't wish you a merry xmas cause I don't think you deserve it. And may u have a miserable 2015 for trying to have it all without consideration how it will affect others than yourself.

Ha ha, I feel so witty. I am quite sure that he will read the irony between the lines and that I am not really that angry at all.

Sorry is not enough

No it is not, I think and smile. Then I see an email from **Gemma Littleton** as I am flicking through the phone. An unread one. What now?! Can she STOP turning up in my FUCKING PHONE AND MY PERSONAL SPACE?!?!?!?? The harmony disappears in one instant. All jolly closing-in-on-Christmas-feelings just vanish.

Just saw that Gemma has sent me an email AGAIN. I'm going to read it and answer her.

No answer back from Dwayne on that one.

To: Andrea Hunter 2014-12-22, 10:06
From: Gemma Littleton
Subject: (no subject)

Hi Andrea, how are you?
Hope all is well in Sweden. Just need your advice on when would be the best days for Dwayne to see the boys. We are looking at booking a weekend probably early Feb. Would it be best to come over on a Friday leaving on a Sunday or come over on a Saturday and leave on the Monday?

But is she for real? And is he for real? Can he actually not handle anything by himself? And does she really think she can be all hubby with me? I almost spit venom as I read the 'We are looking'-words. And oh - is it FEBRUARY now?!

Also, are the boys coming over for the Chelsea game in March?
Apologies if email sounds abrupt (not my intention) rushing
round like a headless chicken at the moment trying to get
everything done before Christmas.

Headless - that's for sure. And she must be very uncertain with Dwayne to try to get confirmation from me. Or is this just a way for her to show me that Dwayne reveals everything to her? To take posit on as THE girlfriend? Maybe she is very uncertain right now when closing in on Christmas - THE BIG EVENT for all parents when it comes to having children together.

I know you must be busy but please try and get back to me as I
want to book as soon as possible.
Cheers, Gemma

Answer as soon as possible? F-o-r-g-e-t about that Gemma. The email gets me fuming. I decide to not answer back. I realize that I probably won't 'be civil' about it. I will think long and hard how to give a grown-up response.

I manage about 24 hours before the fumes suddenly explode into an angry email back.

To: Gemma Littleton 2014-12-23, 10:22
From: Andrea Hunter
Subject: Re:

Hi Gemma!

Sorry for sounding abrupt back.

I have told Dwayne that all he has to do is to tell me that he loves you and wants to spend his life with you, and I will make it easy for you to get a relationship with the boys and be part of their life - but he just 'hmms'. Somehow I don't think he wants his two (if that's all) lives to meet. And he still doesn't call it that you and him are living together. This makes it totally awkward for me and the boys that you are coming. I really really can't understand why he just can't say that he wants to be with you? I couldn't possibly think any less of him. And it makes it hard that he puts us in this situation without strong feelings involved. I really would respect him more if he stood by your side and tried to make things work with you and the boys. Hope you come to your senses when it comes to this man - if you do I'd like to meet you, I think we can have fun together!

I can't let you know what's best this early on - weekends don't get planned until late due to Alexander's football and other stuff. Dwayne will have to come with a suggestion to me and I will let him know if it works.

As for the Chelsea game - boys won't come over by themselves before Dwayne and I have had a talk. And if he doesn't come to Sweden before, then I am going with them to London to talk to him there. And he will pay for a luxury hotel room of my choice.

Cheers,
Andrea

I hope they have a fucking horrible Christmas.

NINETEEN

Birthday treat

"Happy birthday Andrea! Haaap....."

"Urgh. Quick. Bucket. Need to throw up. Noooow-uwaarf!"

My 32nd birthday started a little bit different than the ones before. There had most certainly been a throw up or two in the past due to too much alcohol, but now it was due to a nice cocktail of nitrous oxide, epidural and a baby pressing its head through the spinous. It had taken me 3 days to open 3 centimeters, and 2 hours to open the 7 rest so I was pretty exhausted. The birthday-song that Sophie, my parents and the nurse had tuned up in got abruptly interrupted by me throwing up on the vinyl floor. It was just past midnight, into the Midsummer Saturday, and I had been in and out of the hospital since the Wednesday when my water broke. I had seen enough deliveries on the telly to know what was going to happen after the water broke, but my one didn't seem to follow the usual manuscript. You were supposed to rush off to hospital, driven there by your partner in an extreme hurry, and well in the hospital you were supposed to start panting, screaming, pushing and get wiped on your forehead. Depending on if it was a drama, comedy or thriller your partner would either get a tearful look, a smack on the forehead, get bitten, faint and/or get shot or turned into a werewolf. In my case - none of the above happened.

It was in the middle of the night when I woke up by wetness in the bed, and when I called the maternity ward they asked me to come in for a check-up in the morning. My panties got soaked but more than that - nothing. No pain, no rush, no frantic driving, no partner (as in father-to-be), no nothing. Sophie came and picked me up early to drive me there and I called Dwayne and left him a message. 'My water broke - I'm going to the hospital now'. I hoped he would jump into a plane to try to get here on time by sheer enthusiasm and worry, although I wasn't sure that he wanted to get here in time for it at all. I had asked him about when Sebastian was born and if he was there with his wife in the delivery room. He told me that he had gone there with her and then just left. He said he couldn't face the things going on in there. Since they now were divorced I wasn't sure I wanted him with me in there. I didn't want to be dependent on him and then he would just chuck off. And how would he react with all the blood, sweat and tears - and puke and poo that could also be on the agenda? Would he love me more - or less - if he saw me in that state? I had a romantic illusion that Dwayne would look at me with tears, happiness and extreme love in his eyes after I had given birth to his baby girl or baby boy, but since I was a realist I had asked Sophie to be the back-up plan and stick by me in case Dwayne wouldn't cope, or turn up at all. And I secretly wanted her with me - I was pretty sure that she would be a better support when the going got rough.

At the hospital they noted that I hadn't open more than a centimeter, that the amniotic fluid looked okay and that I could go home again and wait for labour pains to kick in, but that I had to come back in the evening for a check-up. I was a bit disappointed but excited about the fact that the process had started.

When I came home again it turned out that Dwayne must have seen some of the movies anyway. I had loads of worried messages. I called him and calmed him down. He couldn't believe that I was released I didn't ask him about coming over. I just said that this will probably take some time. And he said nothing about booking a flight.

In the afternoon someone called from an un-known number and I heard a gurgling sound in the background. It turned out to be Annabel calling from the hospital, with her newborn second son sucking away on his mothers tits. I got thrilled - soon I was going to be in that position as well! But at the evening check-up there was no progress, but no complications either, so I got sent home again.

The following morning they put some prostin gel on my cervix to try to get some action. Apparently it would work with 'one-for-the-road'-sex, since male sperm could get the cervix to soften, but since I told the midwife that I waited for the father-to-be to fly in from London, she decided to put some gel on - that would work just as well. Imagine how easily replaced a man can be. I got sent home again and called Dwayne.

"They have started me off now so maybe you should think about coming over?"

"Okay, I'll book a flight. When shall I come do you think?"

"I don't know how long this will take, but check up some flights yeah? On Saturday is my birthday, it would be nice if you'd be here by then."

I was quite sure that the baby would be born within the next 24 hours and that we would be home from the hospital at that point. After being in and out of there I felt that Sophie was a much stronger and better support than Dwayne ever would be. He hadn't once said that he wanted to be with me during the delivery, instead he was whining every time I brought it up - 'but I'm no good at that sort of things' - and I didn't want to force him. Sophie on the other hand was very enthusiastic about her task. She stayed by my side when I got back to the maternity ward in the afternoon. I got greeted with a 'now you don't come home until you are a mother!' and I was excited.

I had started to get contractions, and I felt strong and able. I didn't have a birth-plan other than that I was going to drink loads of fluids, have no epidural, and let the body take care of the rest. With my broad hips and strong body and mind I thought I was made to give birth and that I would have a perfect delivery.

"You have opened up another centimeter."

What? After the whole afternoon and evening with regular pains, that I thought I was handling really well, I was expecting that it would soon be time to push. Now it turned out that it was just very week contractions that wasn't getting me anywhere. What had happened to my body-built-for-baby-birth? Somehow it seemed that it was failing me. I got something to sleep on and Sophie got home to rest.

In the morning I got some more gel. I was irritated that Dwayne hadn't come over to give me a 'one-for-the-road' shag. I was pretty sure that his gel would be more potent than this useless one. I begged the nurse for an 1,5 hour permission to leave after lunch since it was the day of the Midsummer celebrations. I went to the place for festivities at the cottage area with Sophie. Bought some raffle tickets and danced to 'Små grodorna' - a song about jumping little frogs - around the maypole to try to get things going.

When we got back my contractions was weaker than before and I got an oxytocin-injection. I had started to get frustrated and impatient, and to d Sophie that I didn't want Dwayne to come over and see me like this. I looked terrible in the white hospital gown and I didn't want to keep up the appearance in front of him. That he would come and perk me up wasn't even in my mind. I wanted him to come over when all of this was finished and maybe in a week or two, when I hopefully would be back on track and in control of things. I had given his number to Sophie so she could call him and give him updates about the progress. And in case something happened to me. I wasn't in the mood to talk to him, I just wanted the pains to go away. Somehow I had forgotten that it was going to be a reward at the end of this. That a baby was actually coming out of me. Since it was such a - for me unexpected - lengthy process, I had started to doubt that I would receive a baby at all.

In the evening of the Friday they started talking about a Caesarian since it was so long since my water broke and since my contractions were so weak, and I wasn't opening up. I got forbidden to drink fluids just in case. At that info I broke down in pieces. Not by the Caesarian as such but because the drinking was what I had used as a mantra. 'Don't forget to drink, don't forget to drink' and now I couldn't. I was just crying and crying, which got me feeling dehydrated and wanting to drink more. At that point Sophie sneaked out with my phone and called Dwayne.

"Hi, it's Sophie!"

"What is going on, is Andrea all right?"

"Oh, yeah, but she wants you to come over."

"I have booked a flight for tomorrow morning, but I wasn't sure I should take it, I haven't heard from her."

"She is quite busy right now, but get the flight."

"Are you sure that she wants me there?"

"Oh, yes Dwayne! She is longing for you. I'll pick you up at the airport."

* * * * * * * * * * * * * * * * * * * *

Christmas Eve, December 24th, 2014

On the morning of the Christmas Eve - the big day for us in Sweden in opposite to many other countries who celebrate Christmas Day - I let the boys open the presents from their father. Both get thrilled. An expensive wrist-watch for Jason and a complete Chelsea-kit for Alexander.

"Go on. Call daddy now and say thank you. And don't forget to tell him to say Happy Birthday to Sebastian from us, it is his birthday."

Alexander goes first and chats away like anything. He had hardly spoken to his father for the last couple of months but anything involving Chelsea always sets him off in a good mood. Except if they lose a game - he is not so jolly then.

Jason also has a long chat with him. When I eventually hear them round up I'm in the kitchen.

"I'll ask her" Jason says and then he calls out "Mum - daddy wonders if you want to speak to him?"

"No thank you" comes my reply.

I can hear my son giggle at something Dwayne says to him.

"Daddy wishes you a happy Christmas, mum!"

"Well, say fucky Christmas to him too."

Both my sons explode in a laughter. I really have to work on my language.

* * * * * * * * * * * * * * * * * * * *

A son is born

At 6.44 in the morning my firstborn child, a son, was born with the help of a suction bell and a determined doctor, that I could swear put a leg on the bed to get support when he started to pull my stubborn son out of me. The last nine hours I only remembered fragments of. My brother Erik and Petronella popped in to say hello, and my parents came to stay for the rest of the event, but while my mother took turns with Sophie to rub my back and wipe my forehead, my father stayed in the waiting room. At one point he came in and informed us that there was a rerun of 'Seinfeld' on the telly if we wanted to watch it but he only got stern looks back. I also remembered a Finnish brusque midwife who powerfully walked in, grabbed my legs and in her broken Swedish she let me know that 'now you are going to push your baby out, and I am not leaving until it's out, one - two - PUUUUUUSHHHHH!!!'. But eventually her shift finished so she left, and the baby was still in my womb.

But now he was here. My beautiful son. I couldn't stop looking at him and sniff his soft hair. He looked like a little space man with his cone formed head caused by the suction bell, and he smelled lovely even if he was smeared in dried blood and vernix.

Round noon a midwife took him out for a check-up and I heard him loudly test his lungs all the way down the corridor. Just as the door had closed softly it opened up again and I could see an armful of long-stemmed deep red roses and behind it...Dwayne! I felt a rush of happiness when I saw his kind eyes and wide smile.

"I'll leave you to it. Now I am going home for some sleep" said Sophie and I formed a 'thank you' with my mouth as I got wrapped into Dwayne's big arms.

"You just missed him, baby. He is gorgeous."

"Was it him in the corridor?" Dwayne asked. "I heard the little man screaming and I instantly knew it was him. Poor fella', he didn't seem happy" he continued with a smile.

It felt so great that he was here, and it felt so right. What on earth was I thinking that he shouldn't be? His presence made me feel calm and comforted, I wasn't on my own with this little creature, we were together in this.

Dwayne was staying for four nights and they were all spent in the hospital. Jason turned a bit yellowish and he had to be treated with some extra light in an incubator for several hours at the time when I wasn't breastfeeding him.

The days on the ward were spent in a haze. We were walking back and forth in the corridors, worrying about Jason, laying in each others arms, changing nappies filled with, first black, then mustard-like goo (Jason's), or blood (mine). The first ever nappy changed on Jason was done by his father (but that was also the only one - Dwayne almost puked at the sight and smell of a filled nappy from that day on). I felt obliged to give Dwayne a blowjob for making the effort of coming over to us and he seemed

197

pleased about that. That he was still at least part of the center of attention. And I felt like a very special woman. Able to give my man pleasure just twenty-four hours after giving birth. I was not going to be one of those women all consumed by her children. I was going to be a sexy girlfriend too. (A possible prospect when you have one child - after a second child it seems more like that the story of the sexy girlfriend/mother is a legend that is told between frustrated men round the campfire. If they want a sexy girlfriend after having two or more kids with the same woman, after sleepless nights, whining, wiping snotty noses, leaving and picking up at nursery, cleaning etc etc etc, they have to get one on the side...oh yeah, right - that is what Dwayne did...).

The third day Jeanne and her husband came to see and gratulate us. It was the first time they met my boyfriend, which of course was a bit odd (but better than some of my friends who STILL haven't met him...).

"Congratulations and HI Mr Big Secret. NICE to finally meet you!" my friend said as she took a long look at the hunk of a man sitting on the bed. She had a weakness for polite chivalry Englishmen after spending a year in London in her late teens. Dwayne wasn't your typical Englishman but it seemed like she liked what she saw.

"Why have you been hiding him, Andrea? He doesn't look that bad at all?"

Like I had said that he wasn't a looker. And I hadn't exactly been hiding him. He had been playing hide and seek all by himself. Her husband looked a bit more suspicious. He and

Dwayne hardly exchanged a word.

"What a cute little baby! Looks EXACTLY like his father!!"

It was quite obvious that Jason didn't look like Dwayne. First of all he was yellow, but apart from that his features were all fair in contrast to Dwayne's dark ones. Now it sounded like Jeanne knew something about our son's origin that Dwayne wasn't aware of.

"It is thanks to our daughter that you now have your son" Jeanne continued chirping away, "so you could actually thank us!"

The fall before, in August or September, Jeanne had come to my flat with her 1,5 month old firstborn daughter and I had held her in my arms. I had said to Jeanne that this didn't feel that strange, meaning that in contrast to holding babies previous times, when it had felt totally scary and awkward, I felt more confident and calm. I did not feel any biological clocks start ticking though, and I didn't feel my uterus tingle. I just said it matter-of-factly, and a bit jokey. I was trying to be nice with my friend, stuck in the baby swamp while I still had loads of party-life ahead of me. But the way Jeanne presented it, it sounded like I had planned to get pregnant. On purpose. Trapping an innocent man. Dwayne gave her a strange look. I knew what was coming. I knew that Jeanne liked the idea of having an influence on fate. I desperately gave her an intense stare to try to get her to shut up.

Now - when my dear, dear friend, realizes that she has said something she shouldn't, she doesn't shut up or change the subject. It hasn't happened in the past, won't happen in the future, and it didn't happen now. She is one of those who tries to r-e-p-a-i-r the damage. And unfortunately just get her friends deeper and deeper out in the quicksand.

"Ah, it is actually not us you have to thank, it is our daughter. Andrea got infected with the baby bug when holding her!"

If looks could kill. Jeanne would have been killed by mine, and I would have been killed by Dwayne's. Or at least severely damaged. He looked like a cloud of thunder. Jeanne was still alive and kickin' and got more stressed and confused by the knife-throwing stares that flew all over the room in different directions.

"I mean, she realized that she was ready for a baby herself when she held her. But not with you. Or, I mean, she didn't know that it would be with you, and…"

It was like letting an elephant loose in a crystal-glass shop.

"Okay! I think visiting time is over actually! Shall we leave the newborn parents darling? Lovely to see you, hopefully we'll see you soon again! Have a nice flight back, and good luck with the baby!"

I loved my friend to bits but thankfully her husband felt that he had to take command of his runaway train of a wife before everything on the shelves would get shattered in pieces. I couldn't even start trying to explain what I had meant myself, it would only had sounded like I was guilty of something. Neither Dwayne or I mentioned the conversation but I always wondered what he made out of it. Honest to God - I did not plan this.

But maybe my subconscious did? Maybe Jeanne was right.

TWENTY

The baby bubble

The summer of 1999 was an absolutely gorgeous summer.
Warm and sunny, and I enjoyed to be in the baby bubble
and just follow my firstborn's rhythm. Breastfeeding,
napping, strolling with the pram. I spent the days at my
parents cottage and in the evenings I walked through the
cottage area with all the gardens exploding with flowers
and scents. Even if the sun was present, Dwayne shone
with his absence, but somehow I was okay with that. I
knew he had loads of work, and I was fully occupied with
the fact that I had someone with me 24/7, and my parents
helped me with all the practical things. They adored their
little firstborn grandchild. Since they got both me and my
brother when they were so young, and already had enough
time to do things for themselves, they now enjoyed being
part of a baby's life again.

When Jason was about 3 months, in September, he finally turned up. Yet again with some of his friends. Not Tom and Crazy Carter, but Rick and some other guys I can't remember the names of. His friends stayed at a hotel close to us. They came here for some partying, but they were happy to meet me and Dwayne's son, and had loads of laughs about Jason's hair that suddenly had gone red, and the constant joke was 'sure his yours?'. The redness only lasted a month, but it was perfect timing...

Some weeks later he turned up again, with Rick tagging along like the previous visit, and a friend I had met before in London. Simpson Littleton. Rick came back to see the Swedish woman he had met the previous trip and was staying with her, but Simpson was short of cash and I asked Sophie to let him stay at her place, and maybe show him around town. I sold in the idea by reminding her of his good looks, and she accepted. She didn't only show him around the town, she also showed him around in the bed and reported back to me that 'he had the most exquisite body and super-soft skin'. Simpson and Dwayne went back to London but Rick stayed with the girl and found a job in Stockholm. How come it was so easy for him to start a new life? Oh yeah. Probably wasn't married already.

* * * * * * * * * * * * * * * * * * * *

January, 2015

After my email to Gemma, and my refusal to speak to Dwayne at Christmas, I don't hear anything from either of them at the start of 2015.

New Year's Eve had been an enchanted evening with all my, by now, divorced friends. I had planned to spend the big night alone with my boys. I stopped fancying New Year's parties after having the best New Year of all times alone with Jason in our Bromma-flat in 2001, when he had been only two and I'd been expecting Alexander. I found out that there was an option to the high-heel stumbling, freezing-ass-off-in-a-tiny-black-dress-night that usually was the case. Little Jason and I had been sitting at the table with lit candles. I had half a lobster and one glass of champagne, and Jason juice and meatballs. After dinner we had gone sledding in the thick snow outside our flat, while enormous white snowflakes slowly worked their way down from the black sky. It had been magical. Better than any party. When Jason had fallen asleep I had watched telly, and at midnight I called Dwayne, who also had been alone in bed watching movies. I felt like we were close. (What did I know - he might have gone out later, it was only eleven his time. Probably his wife number two, the air-hostess that he kept forgetting about, was on a plane somewhere).

This year I was afraid that I would feel like a total failure though. Single, no grown-ups to celebrate with, a leftover.

Alexander stuck by the computer, and Jason would take any chance to sneak out with his friends and shoot fireworks, fingers, hands and god-knows-what of his body. And inhale vodka. After all - he is fifteen. But my friends came to my rescue. Mika all the way from Gothenburg with her three kids, Annabel with her youngest, and Sophie brought her new puppy. There we were - four single women, with our kids and dogs, having a great time indulging lobsters en masse and drinking loads of champagne. Not feeling that anything was missing. Especially not men. It was a perfect night with Dean Martin and Frank Sinatra as the only grown-up male company.

But after that it went downhill.

The boys and I had been over to London early January the year before and now it is a fact: the boys haven't seen their father for a year. I start to get seriously furious and try to focus on something else to not explode. During my days off work I clean out the wardrobe, the closets, the drawers, the boys' rooms. I throw away loads of old or unused things. I clean, clean, clean. Nothing so effective to get some cleaning done as being dumped. When Sophie told me about how she was sorting out every drawer and cupboard in her and her eloped husband's big house I thought she had gone slightly mad - now I am in that phase myself. At least I get something out of my frustration and irritation. A clean and airy house. But it doesn't help. I'm still angry. Most of all I get angry that I don't hear ANYTHING from Dwayne about coming over to see his sons. And have a closure talk with me.

On January 5th I send him a text.

One year since the boys saw their father. Proud of yourself?

I quickly get a reply.

No I'm not far from it

But he does nothing about it. And I get irritated that he doesn't send the monthly payment he is supposed to without me reminding him. When I ask him about the January payment that was supposed to be due by the end of December I get the answer:

I will do it tomorrow it's only 7th hope your well

But no money arrives. A week later I get another text.

Morning hope your well I have done 2 months yesterday as I have been ill

I reply quickly before I start to think too much. I am really trying to not sound bitter and too angry. More jokey, and a 'I-have-gotten-over-it' kind of woman.

Voodoo is working then ;-).
Thank you.

I don't want to be the reason that he doesn't come to see his sons. And my mood really shifts from day to day. When I get a response to my texts or phone-calls to Dwayne I'm fine with the situation. But as soon as he neglects me, everything that isn't dealt with makes me erupt like a volcano, and I throw up big hot lava-streams.

Lol

Well it can't be me keeping him away. But when the hell did he start to use 'lol'??!

On the last day of my days off during the winter-break I decide that I am not going to give a shit about Dwayne and his eventual plans to see his boys. I book a trip to Cape Verde for me and the boys at their February-break, to not risk that I have to wait for him to make a decision of coming over then, or asking the boys to come over to London since they are off school. I am not going to sit home and get frustrated any more. And I am in desperate need for guaranteed sun, pool, perfect beaches and all-inclusive, and really think I deserve it. I start to feel relaxed. I take command of my life.
Then I get an email.
AGAIN.

To: Andrea Hunter 2014-01-15, 22:47
From: Gemma Littleton
Subject: Sorry!

Hi Andrea
Sorry for not responding to your last email - Dwayne told me not to email you back but as I don't like being told what to do I decided to reply anyway!!!
I should not have interfered about visits so big apologies if I upset you - I will be leaving arrangements to Dwayne in future.

I do not want there to be any bad feeling between you and I because despite what he says Dwayne and I are in it for the long haul and sometime in the distant future I will figure in your sons lives.

Let's hope for a peaceful and happy 2015 and let karma do its best (though I think in the karma stakes some of us might come off better than others)!!!!
Take care of yourself and keep in contact (if you want).
Gemma

Now why does she have to be so f-ing nice? It would be easier if I could hate her. I do get irritated of her use of the words 'long haul'. It sounds like something Dwayne has said to her. 'Baby - we're in it for the long haul'. Instead of saying to her 'Baby - I love you, you are the woman of my dreams'. And what does she mean with 'karma'? Is she referring to Dwayne and him being ill, or is she hoping for something bad happening to me? Bitch. I'm thinking that Dwayne and Gemma are the reason why I need an expensive vacation. I send him a text.

Hi! Put in £800 extra before March = 50% of boys cost for a trip we're doing to Cape Verde on their school break end of Feb.

No reason why he shouldn't pay for his sons. He seems to be saving loads of money on non-flights to Sweden. Dick.

TWENTY-ONE

"Let's make an other baby"

In the summer of 2001, Dwayne was going with one of his friends, Dave, to follow the English rugby team, British Lions, on their tour in Australia. Dwayne had played rugby professionally in his younger days, for a Scottish team in Glasgow. From those days he had loads of visible memories: a dislocated elbow, pins and needles in every finger, a damaged vertebra in his neck, scars on the eyebrows and his forehead (but maybe that was from his boxing days), sore ankles and knees And a tattoo on one of his buttocks - a chariot - symbolizing his position as number 8, a big steady tank in wartime. Dave and Dwayne were going to meet up with another friend who lived in Sydney, Simon, and travel around the East coast.

"Can't you meet up with me in Sydney and stay for a week? We can stay at Simon's. Wouldn't it be lovely?"

I was so surprised by his question. I had never thought that he wanted me to join him on a trip that so obviously was a trip with the lads but it didn't take me more than two seconds to say yes and book a flight before he (or I) would change our minds. Jason was about to turn two and I was still breastfeeding him. Just before bedtime, but it was very difficult to stop that last meal since he couldn't fall asleep without it. Since he often had breathing problems when he had a cold I had kept on with the breastfeeding since it was said to protect from asthma, but I must say I didn't really think it helped. To go away for a week would definitely help us break the routine, and it was about time.

Dwayne was going to be away for three weeks, a couple of nights in Bangkok (which made me a bit worried) and join the tour after the first games. I was going to join the second week when they were in Sydney, and then Dwayne was staying for another week after I had gone back home. I was going to be alone for a couple of nights in Sydney when they went off to some games in Melbourne, but I was actually looking forward to that. To have a couple of days on my own, with no baby and no man - I was exited about the thought of having my breasts to myself.

As I went into the cab Jason waved to me sitting in the arms of my mother, with his thick little white bare legs in sharp contrast to my mothers tanned arms. I felt a pang of guilt for leaving him for, in total, almost ten days. But I knew he was in good hands. He absolutely adored my parents and was well familiar with staying with them on his own. And I knew I both needed and deserved this trip.

"Don't come home being pregnant!" my father shouted at me as I closed the door to the cab and I just laughed back and waved. How silly of him.

On the way over I had one night in Bangkok myself, but that was spent in one of the airport hotels. I was keen on seeing my man as quickly as possible.

When I landed in Sydney I was nervous. It was yet again a couple of months since I had seen him last and I wondered if he was going to like what he saw. Breastfeeding for so long, and taking care of a child on my own, had made me really skinny. And since I for the first time in two years hadn't breastfed Jason at night my boobs had taken on enormous proportions during the flight. My hair was long, silky and very blonde, and I wore slim, shiny off-white pants (that I had never been able to wear before or after), a turquoise short-sleeved silky shirt and a thong.

Dwayne gasped as he saw me. And his friends as well. Later he told me that when he had pointed me out to his friends as I came through the exit, his friends had thought that he was pulling their legs and said 'no way, get out of here'. That explained their dropped jaws when Dwayne lifted me up in his arms and swirled me around. I looked stunning. My body had never looked like that before (and for sure never after either). That was my 15 minutes in the spotlight.

I had no doubt whatsoever that I wouldn't like what I saw when my eyes spotted Dwayne. I didn't even think about it. We went straight back to Simon's place and locked ourselves in the bedroom. On the way back from the airport our hands had been all over each other and I couldn't wait to have him inside me. My body had been sent into a shock as I saw him and I felt electrified.

"Can I come inside?" he panted when we finally was in bed entangled in each others limbs.

"Yes, I just had my period."

I just literally had the last day of my period on the plane. As I calculated it probably would be safe all week, but I wouldn't take any chances if Dwayne's sperm was the more viable variety. The later in the week the riskier, but this was the first day, and the only opportunity I would let his swimmers pass the canal.

A couple of days later, when Dwayne's friends once again had been thrown out of the flat so we could have it as our own private love-shack, we were laying nude on the couch (sorry Simon) in each others arms after another love-session. Dwayne looked into my eyes.

"Let's make another baby."

His words warmed me, but I didn't get carried away.

"Dwayne, let us take care of the boy we have at home first" I said, but inside I bubbled with happiness.

* * * * * * * * * * * * * * * * * * * *

To: Gemma Littleton 2014-01-16, 18:52
From: Andrea Hunter
Subject: Re: Sorry!

Thank you for your email Gemma - feels a lot better!
I'm glad you feel that you and Dwayne are strong together - then you can't have any problems with him coming over by himself to see the boys and me I hope! I need to speak to him properly to be able to move on. Remember that you've had that possibility and I was in the same situation as you before this came out into the open.
You've probably heard about the cycle of shock and change:
Phase 1: denial and censure of what changed and trying to act like nothing has happened, trying to continue with business-as-usual
Phase 2: confusion and often irritation and anger
Phase 3: new orientation and creativity in the new situation, to finally reach acceptance.
To be able to move on to the next phase it is important to get information. Talk, to be able to understand. I'm stuck in the confusion phase since I'm not able to talk to Dwayne properly about this. And because he is so avoidant as soon as it gets a bit uncomfortable. Except for the first long talk, when he was just crying and crying, it has mainly been about the boys and as soon as I talk about the serious bits or get angry he disappears from contact for a couple of days 'à-la-Dwayne-style' :-)
I need to sit down and talk with him for all our sakes (and a bit because he will feel VERY uncomfortable to have to stand up for what he has done - that will be revenge enough for me I think :-)
As I said - I definitely don't want him back!

I want Dwayne to make the effort to come and see the boys and at least pretend that he arranged it by himself. I am always extremely irritated by men who are incapable and have to let their women fix things for them. I've always refused to be his 'project-leader' but when it comes to him seeing the boys I've always had to take that part. I'm not doing that any more and I don't want you to have to do it. Sadly I don't think he'll get his finger out.

I wouldn't be surprised if he has asked you to marry him, that would be his style. He proposed to me 3 times and the third time I actually said 'yes' but nothing happened anyway (which I'm glad for now :-). Somehow I don't think you will let him just slip out of his promises :-) Just make sure I know it before the boys though please - otherwise it will be very awkward for them. I will make it easy for you and the boys as long as I get help to move on and get over this threshold that he and I haven't spoken properly, and the EXTREME anger I feel that he hasn't made the effort to see the boys (as I said: I'm stuck in a phase).

I think it's good that you emailed me though he said you shouldn't. He hasn't got a clue what's best and what everyone needs :-)

Have a good weekend and year (and we will keep in touch when needed)!

Andrea

For some reason I want Gemma to force Dwayne to marry her. He will be, and feel, so trapped. To have to marry someone because she doesn't trust him. Serves him right. I have no problem with them getting married. It hasn't stopped Dwayne from doing what he wants in the past and it won't stop him now. And I want Gemma to feel jealous of me, that I had been proposed to by him. I want her to really get the picture that I was special to him. Maybe he has proposed to her as well in the past but then she would probably feel as fooled by him as I did.

I call Sophie after I've pressed the send-button, and proudly tell her what I have written in my email to Gemma.

"Ouch, that thing about him asking you to marry him will probably hurt her."

"You think?" I ask innocently. "Why?"

"Because then she realizes that you were not just a fling, that she probably has talked her self into, and that you were the real thing."

"Hmm, maybe" I say and feel triumphant. "That is just what I want!!" I burst out as I can't hold it any longer.

"Well you probably succeeded" Sophie says dryly.

* * * * * * * * * * * * * * * * * * *

"Marry me"

I was crazily in love with Dwayne on that trip to Sydney, and constantly high on endorphins and oxytocin. We kissed the whole time and held each others hands wherever we went. At one point when he took my face in his hands, put his Paul Newman lips onto mine and let his tongue play with mine, my nipples reacted like over-boiled toffee dripped into a glass of cold water and stiffened in an instant. My clitoris got so blood-filled that I suddenly understood what it felt like to get an erect penis. He skipped one game to be with me and we rented a car and drove to the vineyards of Hunter Valley. Got tipsy as we were taken by horse and carriage between the different wine tasting places, snuggled up by the fireplace at a little bed&breakfast cottage, and ate strawberries laying in bed.

When we came back to Sydney I shoo-ed him off to his friends that were watching one of the games in a bar with a 'enjoy the game - I'll catch up with you later'. I was desperate to just relax on my own for a bit after spending 24/7 with him. I wanted to be with him, but I also needed some alone-time to charge my batteries, and catch up on some sleep since I was still a bit jet-lagged.

"Mmmree!"

I turned around as I was crossing the street and heard Dwayne calling something to me.

"What?"

"Marry me" he shouted again, trying to get heard in the city noise.

"Yes" I shouted back smiling, as I saw Dwayne making a scared face and then started to smile his signature Gene Kelly-smile.

I shook my head laughing and went back to Simon's flat overlooking the Sydney Harbor Bridge. I had always said to myself that if he proposed to me a third time I would have to say yes. That would show that he was eager enough. First time he proposed was in the kitchen of my Bromma-flat when Jason was about one. We were making dinner and he was coming up from behind and asked into my ear.

"Will you marry me?"

"Are you mad?" I had said and turned around. It had come from out of the blue and I wasn't sure that he had asked because he wanted to, or felt obliged to. I wasn't that keen on getting married. I couldn't see the purpose of it, and had always felt that it was some figment to enslave women. And men too for that matter. I was convinced that true love didn't need the chains of marriage to stand solid. And I thought that it would involve too much work once you decided to part.

"We don't have to get married, do we?"

"Well, I've asked you now anyway" he answered and we continued with dinner.

For someone already married it was a strange question don't you think?

Second time he proposed was some six months later in a playground in Bromma. He just casually asked again if I wanted to marry him while we helped Jason on the swings and I just said 'no' and laughed. But the third time...now you can't say no to that can you?

Of course I was pregnant when I came home. The love-hormones in my body, created by the intense infatuation, probably had set my eggs off premature. But it started a bit differently this time.

Two weeks after coming back from the trip my period started like clockwork. I called Dwayne.

"I got my period, so you don't have to worry" I said, quite convinced that he had gotten carried away in Sydney, and as the situation were not really wanted another child.

"That's a shame. Maybe next time" he answered to my surprise.

"It's for the best Dwayne. We are not actually on solid ground here."

I managed to sound cool but my heart did somersaults. 'He wants more children with me!!! He must really love me!'

In the evening I met Annabel for a pre-planned glass of rosé wine in the sun after work. We were supposed to go to the beach bar by the canal, Strandbryggan, but when we finally left work, threatening dark clouds promising thunder loomed above us, and we decided to go to an English pub in Stureplan instead, The Bull and Bear Inn. A suitable place to have a non-stop oneway conversation about the FANTASTIC Londoner I was lucky to be with, over a glass of red and a pint of Guinness. Or two. Annabel lapped up the story of the big charming hunk of a man, like a cat licking milk. After yet another couple of years down the line of marriage the stories of everyday life with husband and two children couldn't match the ones of the juicy bits happening down-under.

The next day I got a bit curious. The bleeding that had started the day before had stopped. It hadn't come that much and I got a strange feeling of déjà-vu. I didn't tell Dwayne straight away. Surely the period had just come in to some sort of hick-up? Maybe the wine and the beer had made some effect. Don't mix red and Guinness? When yet another day had gone by I called Dwayne.

"It is something strange going on. I got my period but it stopped abruptly. It has never done that before."

I couldn't tell if he got irritated or just was busy at work.

"I'm sure it's nothing."

"Well I'm going to do a pregnancy test tomorrow if it doesn't come back soon."

The next day. Different bathroom. Different kind of test-stick. But the same procedure. The same feeling. An instant +. Oh. My. God. No Godmother-to-be to call this time though. It was me. 'I just had my period - come on in'.

When I called Dwayne to share the news he didn't sound happy at all. When I asked him what we were going to do he just said that he didn't know. We agreed that he had to come over within a months time so we could talk about it and make a decision. I was puzzled. What was different from the 'shame - another time' just a few days before?

I came back to that question from time to time over the

years. The only conclusion I could come up with was the one that when it came to Dwayne he enjoyed visions. But when it came to realization of the vision, or getting presented with facts, it wasn't his cup of tea. And now I understand that his wife had probably come back from one of her flights and seeing her made him remember that he was actually married. To someone else than me.

TWENTY-TWO

Number one on the list of what a
woman don't want to hear -
especially not from the man she is
expecting a baby with

Dwayne's eyes were completely black as he stared into mine, and his body shivered as he was clenching his fists hard. He hissed the words through clenched jaws:
"At this moment of time I don't want another baby with you!"

Less than two months after the Sydney-trip Dwayne came to Sweden again. I decided that we would leave the city and go up north, to a cabin my father inherited from his parents, less than three hours drive from Stockholm. I wanted to show Dwayne this beautiful place, the house only 60 square meters, but with a fantastic view of the landscape and literally ten steps down to a lovely, 1500 meter long lake, the Esttjärn in the little Dala-village Nordåker. Nordåker was situated just below some dark green fir tree hills and our little house was the only white one amongst old Falu-red barns and country houses. I wanted us to get away from all the possible disturbances of the city, like shopping and television. Here we were completely in nowhere. We had a serious decision to make. Again.

By then I didn't know that the countryside gave Dwayne the chills. He could appreciate it for a day or two, but then he wanted to go back to the city-buzz. I, on the other hand, would love to stay there for weeks, so we could get back to the cocoon-feeling of his first visits. With a two year old child it was a bit more difficult to just cocoon though...

When we arrived I was so eager to show him the house and the surroundings. The house went really quick to go through. By then it had a simple standard, and just a living room, a bedroom, a kitchen and a small bathroom. I could tell that Dwayne immediately started to think what you could do with this place, since it was so nicely situated. A couple of years later the house was supplemented with a beautiful glazed veranda overlooking the lake, and a balcony, made by my father. He also renovated the kitchen. Sadly Dwayne never got to see it, as we after this first trip never went back together.

After unpacking and putting up the travel-cot for Jason in the small bedroom I wanted us to take a walk round the small village, but Dwayne wasn't that keen. 'I'm not into walking really' he said and that was news to me. I loved walking. And that was part of the plan with the trip up north, to have lovely walks together, with Jason in the trolley. Instead we poured ourselves a glass of wine, and tried to relax. What we should have done was to start some dinner or something. We hadn't really eaten since breakfast, and with the driving, grocery shopping, and getting settled it was way past dinnertime, both for us and for Jason. I was eager to get Jason to bed, so that Dwayne and I could cuddle up and have some time to talk about the fact that I was expecting again, and maybe make some love to feel the closeness between us before we came to a conclusion... but everything went wrong. Jason was too hungry to eat and just refused anything I tried to give him. And since he had slept the whole trip in the car he definitely didn't want to go to sleep - and above all not with an empty stomach. He was getting grumpy and angry and screamed louder with every try for food or sleep. Dwayne tried to calm him down but Jason didn't buy it this time. It was getting later and later. I got more and more frustrated and was determined that he needed to fall asleep to snap out of his fit. I had the experience of what worked and what didn't when my son reached this level of agitation. He looked like the baby in 'The Incredibles' when he got on fire in the end, and I knew we were beyond 'cooing and cuddling'. Dwayne didn't agree with me but instead of starting the dinner, or anything else useful, he began criticizing everything I did. Eventually I burst into flames myself and roared. Both adrenaline and hormones were swirling around in my body.

"YOU ARE NEVER HERE DWAYNE! YOU HAVEN'T GOT A CLUE HOW TO TAKE CARE OF HIM! JUST GET OUT OF MY FACE!!!"

We were standing on opposite sides of the travel-cot in the small bedroom and I was holding a screaming Jason in my arms. Both he and I were covered in sweat and deep red in our faces. It was at that point that Dwayne put his face six inches from mine and uttered the words. 'At this moment of time. I. Don't. Want. Another. Baby. With. You.' He pronounced every word loud and clear and each and every one of them was stabbing me like a knife.

Now. Maybe you have said something yourself in an argument - in the heat of the moment - that you knew wasn't that nice, or maybe downright ugly. Or maybe you have been on the receiving end and heard something that made you really sad or angry, or upset. Then, when you calm down, you know that the one who said it to you didn't really mean it. Or maybe you got the 'sorry' or said it yourself to soften things up. But then you may also know that some words can get etched into your memory, and never get erased. It can get replayed over and over again, long after you kiss and make up.

Amazingly Jason closed his eyes when Dwayne and I

started our oral combat. I just put Jason down in the cot and walked out of the house. I was trembling with anger and stirred up emotions, and was afraid that I was going to kill Dwayne if I stayed. Not with a knife, but with lethal, poisonous words. As I came out in the cool late summer breeze I felt myself calming down. I walked straight out onto the small wooden pier and sat down. Not a sound was heard from the house. I felt upset, but more than that I felt sad. This was it. I could never forgive him for saying those words. If he felt like this we couldn't have another child. We shouldn't. We wouldn't even be a 'we' after this. I sat out there for almost an hour. I tried to imagine how it would feel to finish things, both with Dwayne, and with the pregnancy. I heard the swallows making little noises as they caught insects swarming over the lake. I watched the last bits of daylight turn into a velvety dusk. As small fish created rings on the water trying to catch the water spiders floating around on their feet, and the odd heavy splash was heard from the old pike lurking in the thick reed close to the little beach, I made up my mind. Suddenly I didn't feel angry anymore. Not even sad. I just felt tired. And hungry.

Dwayne was sitting in the dark when I came in. Jason was quiet, blissfully asleep.

"Shall we eat something Dwayne? Are you hungry?"

"Yeah, let's open the crayfish package. They are ready to eat aren't they?"

I was going to introduce Dwayne to the Swedish crayfish eating on this trip. With all the trimmings. I had so much plans for this week. Now we just ate them in silence as we both were starving. And then we went to bed and fell asleep in each others arms, never mentioning the horrible things that had been said between us again.

In the morning as I woke up, still in Dwayne's arms after a full night's sleep and beautiful Jason still snoozing in his cot, I looked into Dwayne's eyes, all hazelnut colored again.

"I can't have an abortion. Not when I know that the thing growing inside of me becomes such a fantastic thing. Hard work, but fantastic. And I love you. It may be difficult, but it is our child. I am going to have this baby."

"I know" Dwayne answered and kissed my forehead. "Can we drive back to Stockholm tomorrow?"

* * * * * * * * * * * * * * * * * * * *

February, 2015

The trip to Cape Verde is just what I need. Just me and the boys. Sun, pale soft almost white beaches. Breakfast, lunch and dinner served with a variety of food so the boys can pick whatever they want. No decision-making whatsoever. And lousy wi-fi so we play poker and Yatzy about twenty times a day. All three of us both win and lose, and get the elusive five-of-one on the dice. That it is a free-access bar and a 12 hour open cafe isn't bad either - if you feel the urge to munch on something between the meals. Not great for the figure though. A massive native woman gives €20 massages that does wonders to my tense body. Although I could have skipped that she popped pimples unasked, and even though the head massage was lovely it was incredibly difficult to get the oil out of the hair since the shower only had warm water between 06.15 and 06.16. In the morning.

While on the trip I decide three things. Life is too precious to stay in limbo.

1. I need to get closure to move on.
2. To get closure I need to see him.
3. The boys need to see their father.

The problem is that I can't get him to come to Stockholm. I haven't managed it in the past, and most certainly I am not managing it now. I need to go to London. With the boys. But I don't want to pay for it. It would feel like a failure that I have to pay for a trip to London to see him, so that I am able to get my closure talk. Which I wouldn't need for a start if he hadn't done what he had done.

Then I realize that I need a fourth thing. I want him to suffer. A plan for revenge starts forming in my head.

1. Kill him. Nah, it wouldn't take many coppers to figure out the prime suspect. Me or Gemma. I've seen enough episodes of Midsomer Murder to know I would get caught. And it would hurt the boys most. Neither father nor mother since I would definitely go to prison and they would much likely never visit me.

2. Withhold him from seeing his sons. No, it would hurt the boys as well. And it would fall back on me.

3. Write a book about this so my version gets known among his friends and acquaintances. And let this man who doesn't think his life is anyones business see his foul-play exploited. Hah! But when would I have time to write it though? Working full time and taking care of two boys and a dog. And someone would have to read the story for it to have any effect.

4. Become a bunny-boiling-bitch. Hm. I like animals too much. Maybe boil his cock? He seems pretty fond of it. Doubt I will get anywhere close to it from now on though. Maybe I can get Gemma to act like the bunny-boiling maniac of 'Fatal attraction'? After all – I'm the one with the kids. In my perspective she is the one on the side, even if she actually has had more one-on-one time and everyday life with him. I could try to drive her nuts. Send her photos of me and Dwayne together – with dates – so that she can picture him in my arms when he had left her after their mutual breakfast to go to work in the past. Or when he had called her from a 'work-conference' and actually was in a hotel with me in Isle of Wight. No woman is able to cope with that. What the hell has he told her??

5. Get in super shape! With even longer legs, perky breasts, pouty lips and go to him and say: "Big mistake. HUGE!" Like Julia Roberts in the Rodeo Drive-shop in Pretty Woman. My God – too much hard work. To start exercising. And the cost for surgery and Botox... I wonder what that Gemma woman looks like? I picture her as a big fat Gemmarrhoid in Dwayne's butt

Everything of the above seems unrealistic. And demands loads of energy that I don't have at this point, or affects the boys in a way that's not right. I start to think that the only reasonable thing is to get him to have to face me and say that he is sorry for what he has done. Since he always wants to take the easy way out that will be hard for him. Right now it feels like everyone has sorted it out for him. Gemma and I have sorted out his relationship: she'll keep him, and I let him go. I have told the boys. His parents now know. He doesn't have to do anything – just carry on with his life as he knows it and bury everything that feels uncomfortable in the back of his head. I want him to know that his way of dealing (or rather not dealing) with this is the wrong way, and that it gives consequences.

Gemma probably hates being alone and single at her age. I don't know how old she is, but by having a 21 year old daughter she can't be that young. Maybe she thinks it is better to be with the man she once chose, instead of getting out . That is her problem, not mine, and I think that for him to be stuck in a sour relationship that he can't get out of is more of a punishment than being alone. I am convinced that Gemma won't be able to just forgive and forget this, and trust him blindly. Surely she must be a bit suspicious of everything he will do from now on? And keep asking him about things, double-checking what he says, doubting his words. He will hate that.

TWENTY-THREE

Knowing me, knowing you

When Dwayne went back to London he told his parents about us. For the first time. And showed them photos of Jason. From his first weeks and up to his second birthday. His mother had burst into tears. I was relieved. Finally we were acknowledged by the London relatives. He also told his parents that we were going to have a second child, expected in April. Not even my own parents had been let in on that secret since it was so early. From that day it seemed like his relationship with his parents was miraculously repaired. I thanked myself, my son, and our unborn child for that. I had been telling him to contact his parents to let them know about Jason. That he had a second child. Now he had finally listened. It was important with family.

I wonder what his mother was thinking about her son getting children with someone else than her second daughter-in-law. Probably she was not only crying about missing out on the first years of their Swedish grandchild.

Dwayne didn't come to the hospital for his third son's birth either. Annabel was the back-up plan this time and she was also extremely dedicated to her task. She loved giving birth. Said it was 'better than sex, more powerful than an orgasm!' and I swear to God - I can NOT agree with her on that.

This time it went quicker, with real contractions before the water broke. But as soon as I entered the hospital in the company of my parents, the contractions disappeared and progress stopped. I took a cab back to my flat alone and promised to call Annabel when it was time.

As soon as I came home late in the evening the contractions started again. I laid myself in the bathtub and tried to endure them. I was NOT going to go in too early again. After a couple of hours the pain was unbearable, but with my lack of confidence when it came to baby-birthing I didn't think I was that far gone at all. I called Annabel for support at three o'clock in the morning. I was panting, I had just had a contraction and had to ask her to hold before I could speak as the pain faded. Then I started explaining that I was afraid to be alone.

"I don't want to be on my own Annabel. Can you come over and beeaa... AAAOOOUUUUHHHAaaaarrrrGHHHöööh..." came out of me as yet another contraction ripped through my body.

"Andrea. Call a cab IMMEDIATELY and go to the hospital.

I'll meet you there. There is no time for me to come and pick you up."

She could be a midwife. I didn't call a cab though. I called my father that had to rush out of bed, being extremely discontent and worried about the fact that I hadn't stayed at the hospital. Annabel met me at the entrance with a wheelchair that she had found in one of the hospital corridors. As I flung open the car door I threw up on the asphalt.

"Good girl!" she cheered. "Right through the spinous process!"

Well in the delivery room I took such a deep inhalation of the nitrous oxide that my eyes rolled backwards in my head and I would have fallen on my back if not Annabel had stood behind me. She was such a support! Except from filming my second son's head coming out between my legs, although she had promised to film only from the waist and up.

Everything went well, apart for some dramatic moments when it turned out that the baby had the umbilical cord around his neck, which caused some disturbance in the room. When my newborn son laid safely in my arms I called Dwayne although it was only about 5 o'clock in London.

"Hi baby. You have got another son" I cooed as I was high on oxytocin and alcohol free cider although I sharply asked for champagne since I thought I deserved it.

"Oh. Okay. Good."

That was it. Didn't he understand what I had been

through? I blamed the fact that he must have been fast asleep when I called and ended the call quickly with a 'get back to sleep baby, we'll speak later'. I didn't want anything to destroy these first moments with my beautiful boy. I would speak to Dwayne later in the day. He would be thrilled then. Now I know that he probably was in bed with Gemma, either in London or in a hotel room in Spain according to her emails, and had to pretend that it was a call from work. Like a pipe that had started to leak, and someone had taken care of it and called to let him know. Well it was true. MY pipe had exploded with blood and amniotic fluid and I had taken care of it. While HE had been in the arms of f-cking Gemma.

When he called round lunchtime he was all lovey-dovey again. And in the evening when he called again, I suggested that we would name our second son after my grandfather. His name had been Alexander Jason Hunter and Jason was already named after him. Dwayne liked the name Alexander - it sounded strong. But he didn't come over to be with his newborn third son. It took him 6 weeks before he finally booked a flight. I was in the baby-bubble and got loads of help from family and friends, but of course I was on the phone begging him to come over to see his boys. But I was also very understanding about the fact that he just couldn't flee the country when waiting for a court date. He had gotten into a bar fight and beaten up a guy after getting a bottle of beer smashed in his head. Of course he couldn't just jump on a plane. Of course I understood. But he was missing out on so much.

When he finally came late in May it was like no time had passed at all. Everything was perfect. Our Alexander was a beautiful happy baby, hardly crying and easy to please. Even the weather showed itself from its most perfect side. 25 degrees, blue skies and loads of sun. Dwayne had a new tattoo on his arm, his left one this time. Some Chinese signs. His boys names, all three of them he said. I was so proud and happy. Alexander looked so tiny in Dwayne's big, tattooed arms, and Jason loved to be with his funny and strong daddy. Although our oldest boy seemed to find his mother quite powerful as well. One day he pointed at the television screen as they were showing the world's strongest man pulling a train with his teeth. The world's strongest man at the time was enormous and had long, blonde hair.

"Look. It's mummy!" he said to Dwayne's exploding amusement. I was not as happy.

I was more happy when we finally went to London, to meet Dwayne's parents. We also met his brother and his wife, and the boys' cousins that were the same age as our boys. Now I wonder if they knew about Gemma already then. For sure they knew about his wife number 2.

No wonder his mother had cried when she heard about us, no doubt not the first time her oldest son had caused her trouble.

* * * * * * * * * * * * * * * * * * *

March, 2015

As soon as I am back from our Cape Verde-holiday, I call Dwayne and ask him if he has gotten the tickets for the Champions League game between Chelsea and PSG in March. I know he hasn't - of course not. 'I was waiting for you to get back to me!' is his answer when I remind him that I asked him to get the tickets already before Christmas.

"Too bad. I thought it would have been a perfect gift for Alexanders birthday i April."

I'm hoping that he will hook the bait. And he does.

"Maybe I can get a ticket for a Chelsea game on Stamford Bridge instead?"

"Yeah - he would love that, Dwayne! Is there any home-games in April?"

I hear him get a bit distant as he checks.

"Chelsea vs ManUnited! I'll get tickets for that!"

Good. Top teams = expensive tickets. Before Dwayne understands it he has agreed to pay for the boys trips, AND mine since that is one of my demands. I am not sending the boys over on their own unless he faces up to me first. And he agrees to pay for a luxury hotel for me.

But he whines. Not about the luxury hotel. At first.

"But what are we going to talk about? What is there to say?"

And then he whines about the cost.

"Please get a reasonable hotel. London hotels are very expensive."

"What? Don't you think I am worth the best? After what you have done?!"

And then he gasps when he hears about the amount of days I'm planning to come over with the boys.

"FOUR DAYS? Why do you have to come for four days? The game is on a Saturday. You could actually come in the morning and then go back on the Sunday?"

During the call I have been fairly calm, trying to keep a light mode, but now I snarl at him.

"Dwayne! You haven't seen the boys for ONE YEAR and THREE MONTHS by now, how can you even suggest that 24 hours could be enough?!"

He shall be happy that I didn't ask of him to get me a house so I can move to London.

PART 3.

THE CLOSURE TOUR

TWENTY-FOUR

Mission possible

"Mum, you're not going to do something bad to daddy, are you?"

"What?"

I get puzzled by Jason's question. It s in the middle of April and time for our trip to London. I sure as hell am very determined to get my closure talk. Especially when Gemma informed me that he 'doesn't do closure'... I always love a challenge. And I need the closure talk to be able to move on. I'm trying to be calm about the trip and meeting him again, and try hard not to stress myself up. To stay sane, I write down every question I can think of, that I want an answer to from Dwayne. This is the first time I will meet him after everything got revealed eight months earlier. I am trying to not agitate myself at the fact that we haven't seen each other for over a year. One year, three months, two weeks and four days to be exact. And during that time

Dwayne hasn't made any effort to see his sons. Or me for that matter. Wether I shall try and meet up with Gemma or not on this trip is a too big question for me to handle without getting a total meltdown. I decide to deal with that when I come to London. I have booked a hotel close to where I think she lives, if I should fancy trying to see her. In Chelsea, close to South Kensington. Very expensive hotel. And a very expensive area. Fuck Gemma. And Dwayne. Searching frantically on different combinations of Gemma Littleton + London made me come to the conclusion that I had found the right postcode. But Dwayne is paying for the hotel, at least half of it. I don't want to be a total bitch.

"Well, you are not going to kill him or something like that?"

"Ha ha, Jason, of course not. Though I must say it has crossed my mind" I continue and give him a wink, hoping he understands the joke.

"Because, you know, then we wouldn't have neither a dad or a mum, and I wouldn't want that."

Bless him. He has done some thinking. And probably seen too many movies.

"No, I don't want to kill him. I love him. He has given me you boys, and that is the best thing that has happened to me. I love him as a person, but I hate what he has done."

"He might be really sad and sorry, more than you know, and if you are mean to him he might not be able to cope."

I doubt that. He is really hiding it well in that case. But I understand why my son is worried. From movies, tv and internet you hear more about suicide than you need to. But I know Dwayne would never top himself. He would never

242

be able to make the plans for it.

"He might be sorry Jason, but he has a habit of sticking his head in the sand, and let his problems disappear."

"But what ARE you going to do then, mum?"

"I just want him to face me and to say that he is sorry. And answer some of my questions. I need that to be able to move on. I am not letting him stick his head in the sand on this one. He has to face up to me and what he has done."

"Hmm."

Jason doesn't seem that convinced.

Finally on the airplane. I am a bit speeded. Despite my main goal to keep calm, I realize that I am a bit tense. I know, because before I left the house, my father came over to see me.

"It is a hell of a mission you have ahead of you."

I had stopped packing my overnight bag a bit startled. None of my parents had uttered a word about my forthcoming trip to London. I was touched that my father had realized that this was tough for me.

"Yeah, it is a bit stressing yes" I had answered. Like the calm, cool and grown-up person I am.

"Just don't make a big thing out of it. What has happened has happened, no point in digging in it."

It had been at that point I understood that I was a bit tense. After all.

"SO YOU THINK THAT I SHALL PRETEND THAT NOTHING HAS HAPPENED?! LIKE IT'S NO BIGGIE?!!! JUST LET HIM GO ON WITH HIS LIFE? LET HIM GET REWARDED FOR

NOT DEALING WITH IT??!! IS.THAT.WHAT.YOU.ARE.-SAYING??!!!"

It was a good thing that I got it out of my system, because now on the plane I am totally calm. I'm joking with the boys while discussing different scenarios when meeting Dwayne. Like 'shall I throw myself on the floor begging him to take me back?', or 'shall I pretend that nothing has happened and just kiss and hug him like usual? Just say 'I love you'? They laugh at all the alternatives, but say that I shall just be myself. I say to the boys:

"Listen. I've told daddy that I don't think you shall meet Gemma on this trip. That it should be about you and him after all this time. But if he wants you to meet her, and if you feel okay about it, I don't have any problems with that. Then I think you should. But I don't want you to hide it from me."

"I'm going to say that I'll do it for a thousand pounds" Alexander says cockily.

"Yeah, do that" I laugh back. Thinking it is a bit different from in the beginning when he said that he would never want to meet that slut.

Seeing him again

The plane lands half an hour early. Very strange. How can a two and a half hour flight suddenly take only two hours? I almost expect Dwayne not to be there yet, but he is.

His reaction when he sees Jason is expected. He has developed into a young man since Dwayne saw him last. He gives them both a big hug but is giving his attention to Jason. I walk up with a big smile, put my cheek next to Dwayne's and hug him with a 'oh, I've missed you so much'. He gives me a funny look but is returning my smile, halfheartedly. He puts his arm around Jason and walks off, Alexander getting behind. I can see that he is watching his older brother and father chatting easily, and is thinking of his options. Then he starts to walk a bit faster, coming up beside them and lets his arm bump into Dwayne's, as by accident. His father turns to him and starts chatting.

To me it is a heartbreaking scene. In my eyes Dwayne was at first ignoring his youngest son. But instead of getting angry I realize that Dwayne is nervous. It is so easy to focus on how big Jason has gotten. How he has developed into a young man, going from the age of 14 to nearly 16 since his father saw him last. But Jason and Dwayne have talked a lot these past months, and frankly it is Alexander that needs his attention now, more than ever. Dwayne really hasn't got his emotional tentacles out, I'm thinking. He never has. I wonder if he ever had emotions at all. Or if it is a female thing noticing stuff like this. I try to think that Alexander will get his time tomorrow, at the game.

In the parking lot we climb into Dwayne's Cadillac Escalade. I feel a sting of irritation that he drives around in such a flashy, expensive car, whereas I am stuck with bus, underground, bike and my own legs. And I also realize that if Dwayne had moved to Sweden he would never have

245

been able to make himself a career-platform enabling him to have a Cadillac as his company car. No wonder he stayed here in London.

I let Jason sit up front with his dad, as a conversational ice-breaker. Alexander sits with me in the back, a bit quiet, still affected by a migraine outburst last night. Maybe he is stressing about this trip as well. We do our usual tour to Kentucky Fried Chicken - we are just crazy about those juicy chicken legs and take every chance we get to have them - and everything goes smoothly. The regular chat and banter. Dwayne talks about his friend Crazy Carter, that the boys have met several times before, and I suggest I contact him for a drink to let him spill the beans. He answers with a laugh and 'I think all the beans are spilled already'. Imagine that it is so easy to talk in code about something difficult. How familiar everything feels although everything is different. The song with the phrase 'nothing has changed but everything is different' pops into my head. I am also familiar with the feeling of non-excitement when I meet Dwayne. Like it has been for the last couple of years. I really have to admit this to myself. The thrill is gone.

After KFC I say to Alexander that it is his turn to sit up front. He seems very happy about it and chats away with his daddy. When we arrive in Putney, at his parents' address, I have to remind me that he actually doesn't live there. He opens the trunk and pulls out an overnight bag and it gets so real. How come I haven't thought about that before? It is the same bag as always.

TWENTY-FIVE

The closure talk

He fumbles with the GPS, and as it refuses to take the address to my hotel, I can see that an irritation builds up. Not a good start for a conversation - any conversation - and sure as hell not this one. I am thinking of the numerous times I have rehearsed 'take a deep breath, take 10, don't let your emotions get in the way for what you need to say'. I sit quiet as Dwayne finally starts the car. I refuse to get carried away in his anger of 'Miss GPS'.

We have dropped off the boys at Dwayne's parents. His father had met us at the door and after a hug and a kiss on the cheek, his 'how-are-you' was quickly followed by a long rant about the weather, both in London and in Sweden. And all the countries in between. Dwayne's mother had been in bed, having one of her deep chest infections ('absolutely not caused by the constant smoking'). She gave me a hug when I popped up to see her, and asked me if I didn't want to stay with them instead of in a lonely hotel. I just answered that 'it will probably be awkward for Dwayne' and although she said that I should ignore him, I feel that I need my own space. I am sad when I leave them. Wondering if we ever will stay under the same roof again. Despite all, I really like them. Smoking or non-smoking.

"So Dwayne, when this came out in the open" I finally say when the car has passed Putney Bridge, into Fulham and then taken some turns off towards Chelsea. I take a deep breath and ask the question I've repeated to myself, over and over.

"Why didn't you just rush over to Stockholm and tried to repair the relationship with me?"

"What do you mean? We didn't exactly have that sort of communication then."

"Why did you let me get all the information from Gemma? Why didn't you talk to me about it?"

"I didn't think you needed it. You were emailing back and forth with Gemma, and after you found out about everything I didn't think you ever wanted to talk to me again."

He misinterpreted me. I meant 'why didn't you choose me'. But I don't manage to explain it. Not even to myself. When you know it's going to hurt when you bang your head in the wall, it is no wonder that you don't pursue.

"So tell me how it started" I say instead.

"What started?"

God. It's like trying to wring milk from a cheese.

"You and I were together, and you were here in London.

248

How did it start with you being with someone else?"

"I, I, it's... I don't know Andrea. I honestly don't know. I don't know what to tell you" he says bewildered, like he is surprised himself.

I sit in silence. Expected answer number one. I know him so well. And still not at all. Breathe. 1-2-3-...let him do the talking.

"You were there and I was here, it just happened."

8-9-10-11...

"I can't explain it. I'm an asshole and a prick, Andrea. And I can't change what happened."

"Well I know that Dwayne, but let me jog your memory. I was pregnant with Alexander, and rushing back and forth to hospital with Jason with his asthma attacks - sometimes in the middle of the night. I even went in an ambulance with him, eight months pregnant, when he had fever cramps..."

"I know you did" he says quietly.

"I was ready to give birth to our second son, and what happened here in London? While I took care of everything at home? How did it start?"

I can see in his face that this is a bit uncomfortable for him.

"Well, I don't know. It happened once. Then again. And then everything just spiraled out of control to tell you the truth..."

That will be a first, I think to myself.

"...and I was struggling with what to do. Should I move to Sweden, should I stay here."

"Why didn't you break up with me?"

"I tried to juggle things, and I let it go out of hand. I seem to have an issue with upsetting people. I don't want anyone to get upset and along the way that is what I am doing. Don't forget that I have let someone down here as well."

Now, WHY would I care about that?! I think it, but I don't let that take overhand and I continue.

"You should have broken up with me Dwayne, and in my book you haven't broken up yet, so that is what you are going to do during this talk."

"What's the point...bla bla blah, blubb jdjpooi€#)?(/%"/% ()!)blaaah...."

Really - the way he is trying to wriggle out of this is totally in gibberish in my ears.

"You need to do it properly, so I can move on" I say firmly and then change the, well not the subject, but the angle of my attack.

"Your tattoo on your left arm, what does it mean?"

"You know what it means Andrea."

"Tell me. Tell me what it means."

"You know what it means."

How can it be so difficult to say it to me?

"I need for you to tell me what it means Dwayne. Now tell me."

"It means Gemma."

He is really mad, I'm thinking. How can anyone be so stupid and tattoo a woman's name on his arm?? Even if in Chinese? He must have been crazy. Or crazy in love. It hurts. Really cuts into my heart. I was crazy in love with him at the time he made the tattoo.

"And what did you tell me it meant?"

"My boys' initials."

I wonder if he remembers this, or if Gemma has let him read my emails. And then I'm hoping that he hasn't told the boys what he told me. I can see them before me, with their little fingertips following the pattern of the blue ink. 'What does it mean daddy?' 'It's your name my boy, and your brothers'.

I snap back to reality, seeing people outside the bars and the pubs. Friday night happy people, with no problems in the world right now. But wait 'til tomorrow...

"I really wanted to be with the boys, but I didn't want to move to Sweden. My life is in London, and the long-distance didn't work for me. Maybe I was a bit afraid that you wouldn't let me see the boys. Now I know you wouldn't do that" he adds quickly when he sees my angry stare, as he knows that what he just said is not true "but I was afraid to lose contact with them."

Suddenly I can see the name of the street where the hotel is supposed to be. Already? I know it is one of the first houses as we enter the street but I let him drive for a bit longer. As the numbers get higher and higher I finally say that he is going in the wrong direction. He turns around and I tell him to just park the car for a bit. He does, but he doesn't turn off the ignition. Eager to just sprint off. He is staring out of the window.

"Why don't you and Gemma have any kids together?"

I am very curious about that. Gemma only have one daughter, surely she must have warted another child with

Dwayne if she loved him and wanted to be with him.

"I didn't want any more kids" he answers rapidly. "I have three beautiful sons, that is enough."

Then he continues, all of a sudden very angry. I can feel the heat coming from his skin.

"What is the point of all this? I'm tired of talking about it. I've talked and talked and talked. I know I have upset people. You, Gemma, her friends. And your parents and your brother, who are lovely people. They're probably angry with me as well. I want you and me to be able to be friends and this is destroying it! I'm getting really angry and tired now. It's late and it is one hell of a time to have this talk - it is bloody ten o'clock. I don't want to come home to the boys all upset!"

"DON'T pull the 'for-the-sake-of-the-boys'-card on me!" I burst out. "I haven't had a chance to talk to you about it. And you wouldn't come close to me for the rest of this trip if you knew we would talk about this! This is my only chance to get closure. You will stay here until I'm finished so I can move on and we can put this behind us. You have talked and talked and talked with Gemma, but not with me!"

"Well I've told her to shut-the-fuck-up about this as well" he yells, "or I'm off! Hell, I'll disappear from both of you, and neither of you will ever see me again!"

I'm baffled. I wonder why Gemma still wants to be with this man. How can anyone settle for this kind of neanderthal-behavior? In this century? Like he is doing us a favor by being in our lives. We sit in silence for a bit. I'm counting - not stars unfortunately, but seconds - and he is fuming.

"Hell, I probably had the heart attack because of this."

"You think? Of course it is" I say and wonder again if he has read my emails, or if Gemma used my thoughts while talking to him.

"When you were about to move to Stockholm - had you and Gemma broken it off then?"

"I don't know! Why does it matter? Gemma and I have always been on-and-off! I decided to have a go for a life in Sweden. But I couldn't do it Andrea. I couldn't do it. My life is here - in London."

He gave it a chance for in total four weeks.

"How can Gemma stay with you through this?"

"She wants to be with me. She has dwelt with this and moved on. OK, shoot. Let's get it over with!" he says impatiently.

"Now is the time to finish with me. So here I am, all of this has happened. What do you need to say to me? And look into my eyes when saying it."

He spins around.

"Okay, we're finished! We're history! There you go!" he blurts out, looking both angry, embarrassed and irritated. But not sad.

"That wasn't that hard?" I say. And then I continue.

"Well I have lied to you once. I said I hadn't had sex with anyone else since I met you, but I had."

"I knew it."

"After I met you the first time here in London, we went to

Dublin and I met a fantastic man, Johnny O'Reilly, and he was a love-God."

Very silly of me mentioning his name, and bringing him up at all, but it is all I have and I want it to eat into his brain. Like Gemma's name has done into mine, even if my twist of the truth was like a drop in his ocean of betrayal.

"I don't need to hear this. Actually I'm bored!"

What an extremely silly thing to say for a man that has let me chew up the fact that he has shagged someone else for 12 years. Or 16 if he had sex with his second wife that I didn't know about. Which I assume. I am enjoying it. His reaction tells me the thought is eating him.

"But I didn't have sex with anyone after you and I started to have sex, when you came to Stockholm."

"And I didn't have any orgasms with you." I continue. "I faked it. I know you think I just say it to get back at you but it is true. And I have to get it off my chest. You could get me crazily excited but not get me to come. You are actually not a great lover, too impatient and selfish."

"Well lucky you had met Mr Love-God then, that Johnny O'Reeeeeeilly" he says with a funny look on his face.

I can see that it eats him. Serves him right. Revenge, even a nibble, can taste good.

"But it was just a one-off, only that one time. I also want you to call Kate so that I get a confirmation that she knows about the boys."

"Okay - I call her tomorrow. I just have to talk to Sebastian about it."

I know he won't call her but I understand that Sebastian

needs to be prepared. I will have to figure out another way to get it confirmed that Sebastian's mother knows about his half brothers.

"And I want you to tell Alexander that Gemma didn't know about him until recently. It is better that you tell him how that happened with your own words. It is bound to come out sooner or later, and it is not dramatic at all if you just tell him, but it will sound a lot worse if it comes out elsewhere."

"Okay, I understand that. But then I will have to introduce them to Gemma."

"Not on this trip Dwayne. This trip is about you and the boys. You haven't seen each other for a very long time."

"Okay. Anything else?"

I'm trying to think if I'm satisfied with what I have gotten. Can I put this behind me from now on? Leave the past and move forward? I realize that there is one more thing.

"It feels a bit difficult for me Dwayne, because all you are talking about is that you didn't want to move to Sweden, and that your life is in London. I never asked of you to move. I was happy having a long-distance relationship. You don't say anything about that you want to be with Gemma.

"Well I do want to be with Gemma."

There. Finally. Couldn't he have said that in the first place? Already in our first conversations, when this came out?

"It didn't work for me to have a long-distance relationship. My life is here, and I want to be with Gemma. I love the boys madly. Hell, I don't even know if they are mine. But it

255

doesn't matter. I love them to bits anyway."

Why does he have to say that? He is being a jerk.

"Don't say that, you know they are yours."

"Yeah?"

I put my hand on his arm.

"Dwayne. Don't be like that. There is absolutely no doubt that they are yours."

Then I feel a pang of sadness. He wants to be with her. He has always wanted to be with her. Tears starts to prickle in my eyes.

"If you knew that you didn't want a long-distance relationship, how could you keep me thinking we had one. I could have met someone that loved me for real. You wasted some of the best years of my life. It has been going on for so long."

Now the tears are in free fall as I'm thinking of all the could-have-beens.

"I'm sorry for doing that" he says looking sincerely sorry. "I wasted Gemma's life as well."

I SAID - I DON'T CARE ABOUT GEMMA!!!! Or - no - I didn't say it. But I thought it. Can he really not read my mind?

"You were not that fun to be with Dwayne. We have had good times but you really could be an asshole sometimes, which I put up with since we were together. But most arguments we had was because you kept me on an arms-lengths distance. We could have had it a lot better together" I say bitterly.

"I knew what I was doing was wrong. It probably reflected how I behaved. I'm sorry."

So, he could have been a nicer man to be with as well. It isn't his personality, it's the circumstances. Which of course is caused by his personality. But still. I wonder if Gemma got both the cherries and the pie. And I got the crumbles. It hurts. Why didn't I leave him? Why did I settle for a man that at times acted loving and caring but at other times was being a jerk? What I had seen of other relationships around me didn't tell me that I was doing the wrong thing. It is good and bad between couples. Does that mean that everyone lives in a lie? A made-up life of what you want, and only when the shit hits the fan - or a life changing event occurs - only then you have to deal with it and move on?

"Look - you are a lovely lady and I'm sorry I did this to you. You'll be happy to be rid of me. As you said yourself - I wasn't that fun to be with. Things will be different from now on. Boys can come over as much as they like. And Gemma and I will come to Stockholm."

'Lovely lady?' Like he had met a nice lady at the office. Or in a shop. Was that all I had been to him? And the thought of seeing him and Gemma together makes me shiver.

"Was that all? Shall I help you with the bag?" he says, eager to get out of this.

I get an urge to be alone, to lick my now full-open wounds.

"Okay" I say and wipe some of the tears from my cheek.

He helps me out with my bag, looking remorseful. Saying 'I call you tomorrow, we'll do something' and quickly gets back into the car. He really can't take it when someone is sad. Why would I want to see him tomorrow? He should be with the boys now. I have my own plans for this weekend. I walk off to the entrance to the hotel but my tears are blurring my vision. I stop and try to wipe them off with one of my gloves. Why didn't I have a tissue? Did I really think I could get through this conversation without spilling any tears? Dwayne still sits in his car. When I'm standing in front of the hotel door I realize that I have to calm down and get my face sorted. I can't check-in like this. I wipe away the last bit of tears and look for a mirror in my bag.

"The entrance is just there!" Dwayne calls out.

Does he really think I don't know where I am going? 'Just go' I visualize with an impatient waving arm. He starts off, and after a couple of seconds hesitation at the crossing - probably not reflecting if he has made the wrong choice and should turn back to me, but just checking that another car won't smash into his - he is off.

Once in the room I throw myself on the bed. I have no energy left. It is late. I want to call Sophie but it is another hour onwards in Sweden so before I am able to sleep I go through the content of our conversation over and over. And I write it down.

TWENTY-SIX

Lovely lady

Of all the things that could make me cry in the early morning the next day, it is 'lovely lady' that gets stuck and makes my eyes flooded by tears. He didn't call me a 'lovely woman'. A lovely woman that someone someday will love. Not even 'lovely girl', which I was at the time we met. No, a 'lady'. To me that sounds like someone that has passed the expiry date. Marking a distance. A lady in a shop, or at the office, can be lovely. He probably doesn't call Gemma a lady. My tears just keep on coming. I feel so old. Who am I kidding. Who wants to be with me? A lady. I might just stay in the hotel room for the rest of this trip. Why make the effort to go out and meet people? At all?

A good thing that they have tissues by the bed. One after one they get soaked. Here I am in a comfortable double-bed. The tissues are probably there for someone to wipe sperm and sweat off your lover, I reflect bitterly. Not to wipe the tears of a long overdue lady laying here on her own. A Miss Marple.

I realize that I probably haven't had enough sleep. And that I am also in need of food.

Acceptance. My youngest son has the best day of his life ahead of him. I will have to try to think about that, and that it is thanks to me and Dwayne together that it is coming true, even if we are not a couple any more. I come with the ideas and he pays for them...

I get a long, warm shower and walk down to Kings Road. I'm trying to find the perfect café for my mood. Finally I find it. Through the big windows I can see plump white leather chairs, and robust metal tables. 'Ca'ppuccino' is the name of it. When I come in I can see that all the nice plump white leather chairs are occupied. The waiter points down a dark staircase and says that it is more tables downstairs. I definitely don't want to miss the opportunity to look out the window, but as I am now starving I walk downstairs. Immediately I feel that it is wrong. But I can't stop myself. I find a hard wooden chair down there and sit down.

Why am I doing this? I don't want to be in a basement. Luckily it is one of these places where it takes some time to get served. Or maybe it is because I am alone. Suddenly I get up. I can have an influence on this. I can't affect the fact that Dwayne has done what he has done, but I certainly can sit wherever I want to. Or leave. As I come up the stairs there is miraculously a whole table with two chairs available. On the best spot! Facing the window! I slouch down on the cushioned chair and feel very content. I do take charge of my life! I order a large cappuccino, an Egg Benedict - with both smoked salmon and steamed spinach - and a large freshly squeezed orange juice. Treating myself. I wonder why I can't be one of those women who can't eat when they are miserable. So they lose loads of weight and get that famished look. My appetite never fails me. Never.

When the Eggs Benedict arrive they look absolutely delicious. The poached eggs are perfectly shaped and the hollandaise sauce is embracing them like a soft, pale yellow blanket. When I bite into it I feel sheer joy. They are perfect, and the salmon and spinach adds the extra saltiness to it. I look out the window and see the blue sky above the Chelsea houses. Red double-decker buses are passing on the street, very London-ish. I take a sip of the intense yellow orange juice and think that it is strange to move from sorrow and darkness to something totally different. All on my own. I wonder if I did the wrong thing last night. To pick on an open wound instead of letting the thin flesh that had started building up be. It was damn painful to hear that it had been Gemma all along, but now I don't have to think that I could have acted differently or done anything in the past to change the outcome. I should have broken up earlier, yes. But all the things we have experienced have been fantastic. Sure - the memories are a bit soiled, knowing what I now know. But still. We have had some good times, and some bad times. I wouldn't want to be without them. Thanks to them I am the person that I am today.

I feel very serene as I sit there, sipping my cappuccino. But I'm not more than human. The feeling of being Miss Marple - emphasizing the MISS - makes me want to have a face lift. Or at least turn back time when it comes to wrinkles. I write down anti-wrinkle cream on the top of my shopping list.

Golden boy

I must have been an open target as I left the coffee-place. A man calls me as I pass a shop with tempting gold letters on the window.

"Want a free sample of the golden face cream?"

Normally I just look the other way when someone tries to 'offer' me something. I have a contact allergy against sales people. But now I am not myself. I feel invisible and am grateful that someone is noticing me. As I grab the small plastic envelope he says 'You have beautiful skin miss, come let me show you' and I'm stuck. Well in the shop he puts a mirror in my hand and starts smearing me with 'collagen and antioxidants and anti this-and-that'.............

I can see the lines in my face miraculously disappear. It is like magic. Is this what everyone does? According to the salesman 'yes'. But then I start to realize that he talks about serum for several hundred pounds. 'But they'll last for a year, miss!' and some even 'for two years!' (and then you are talking four figures). I can't get myself out of the chair. In the mirror I look younger and younger for every minute and every stroke he places on wrinkles I didn't even know I had. God, I must have looked like a hundred years old before. No wonder that Dwayne called me Miss Marple. The salesman is dancing around me in his tight black t-shirt and gold bracelets, as he keeps explaining the different qualities of the jars in his well manicured hands. He gets wrinkles to disappear round my ears, my eyes, and - my neck?

"See these rosy cheeks you've got. I can make it disappear in an instant!"

He starts rubbing a gel on my left cheek and it feels like little grains of sand peeling me. Probably the gold. Is that really the right way to treat rosy cheeks I'm wondering but he interrupts me in my thoughts.

"Just wait a couple of minutes and you'll see how beautiful your left cheek will be!"

He is incredibly enthusiastic as he then turns to my, according to him, spotty hands. I have never seen any spots on them before, but now I do. Several. Maybe billions. When a couple of minutes have passed I feel like I have to interrupt him.

"Excuse me, I think my left cheek actually has gone a bit redder than my right."

"Hmm, yeah. That is strange. Are you allergic to something?"

"Eh, no. Not that I know of anyway. And it is burning. Can I get the mirror back please? It feels like I have something in my right eye also. It really hurts."

"I will get you some water" he says and then disappears in to a little room in the back.

Christ, the itch in my eye gets worse and worse. And from looking 15 years younger just five minutes ago, I now look like I am a crackhead.

"Here. This will calm you down" he says as he brings the glass of water, and I wonder why I need to be calmed down. Sweat is running down the salesman's forehead and I think that he is the one who needs to be calmed down. He has called one of the other persons in the shop to have a look at me. She looks very bored and potent at the same time. Probably in charge of the shop.

"Are you allergic to something?" she asks with a patronizing glance.

"No" I say and feel guilty for having destroyed their day. "Not that I know of anyway. And not before today" I add sourly.

"Shall I clean it off?" the salesman asks his boss who says 'yes' very impatiently.

"I feel so sorry for you miss. Let me make it up to you. I will give you a free half hour - no let's say 45 minutes - of facial treatment because of this. You can book any time you like. Look here at the computer, we are so fully booked, but I will make time for you."

I start to think that I can kill almost an hour of this trip getting a facial, when he adds:

"All you have to do is buy one of the creams to get the free treatment. They are from £250 and up."

'Only have to buy a cream for £250'? Was this a scam? Did everyone get an 'allergic' reaction? And felt that they had done a good deal spending several hundreds of pounds on a cream to get a 'free' treatment?

"Sorry, I think I need to think about this for a day. And I am actually leaving London in a couple of days, and I guess you're not open on Sunday, and..."

"We are always open! I have been here for 7 days a week for 8 years, and please just look here in the computer, you can get any time you like if you only buy this product. It is solid grains of gold. Here, look! Please!"

I feel like I am stuck in glue and have to fight myself off to get to the entrance of the shop. The mans friendly eager face suddenly grows snooty as he realizes that his prey has just escaped. He waves me off with a 'you can come in any time' and I can see that his manager is throwing him a murdering look. Shame. I really looked the part for a moment.

'I wish nothing but the best for you'

When I am on my way back to the hotel I pass the Market Place Restaurant. It is a lovely day and I decide to go back there in the afternoon to have a glass of rosé. It is a bit early even for me to start drinking at noon, especially after just having breakfast.

When I come back a couple of hours later it is packed of course. A sunny Saturday in April, and actually the first warm day all year, it is bound to be packed. But I am determined that I shall sit in just THAT outdoor restaurant and have a glass of wine, and maybe a greek salad as well. I shall take charge of my life. After waiting in line for 45 minutes I finally get a table. In the shade. I don't mind at that point, and from my shady position I can watch the people around me unnoticed since everyone else has got the sun in their eyes and can't see me. Everyone is in pairs or in groups, laughing and chatting, and seem to have no troubles at all in their lives. The main part is younger than me but some of them could be my age. I can not see any man I fancy though, or would like to chat with, if it would have been possible to break in to any of the conversations round the tables. My options had been narrowed down by my boys also. Jason had asked me to find someone in the music business, so I could help him get famous. And Alexander wants me to meet someone with contacts in the Chelsea team, so that he could get a (football)foot in there. The best would be, according to him, if I shacked up with Didier Drogba, but I'm not sure he has got anything to do with music agents.

As I'm sitting with my longed for glass of rosé, I start to notice the lyrics of the music playing in the background. 'Sometimes it lasts in love but sometimes it hurts instead'. How true. I listen more closely. It is Adele singing with her emotion-filled powerful voice.

'I hate to turn up out of the blue uninvited
But I couldn't stay away, I couldn't fight it
I'd hoped you'd see my face and that you'd be reminded
That for me it isn't over'

Hmm. Was it like that? Wasn't it over for me?

'Never mind, I'll find someone like you
I wish nothing but the best for you too
Don't forget me, I beg
I'll remember you said,
Sometimes it lasts in love but sometimes it hurts instead

Nothing compares
No worries or cares
Regrets and mistakes
They are memories made
Who would have known how bittersweet this would
taste?'

Memories made. Yeah. We have had a fantastic time, and
produced lovely children. And I have loads of nice
memories. But now it is over. No point in hating him,
what's done is done. And I don't want him, so it is no point
in hating Gemma either. Hah! Imagine what a glass of rosé
in the sun can do to your mind! A lot cheaper than therapy!

'Never mind, I'll find someone like you
I wish nothing but the best for you too...'

In the afternoon it is time for Alexander's big birthday event. The Chelsea home-game against Manchester United. I am supposed to meet up with Dwayne and our boys outside the stadium and take Jason while Alexander gets some valued alone-time with his dad, watching their favorite team. I'm trying to not get irritated and bitter by the fact that in 13 years Dwayne hasn't taken neither his second nor third son to a football game, but no doubt his firstborn. And when he finally takes his Chelsea-devoted youngest one, it is I who make it happen. But bitterness doesn't make wonders to your appearance, I have to stop thinking ugly thoughts. The redness on my cheek and in my eyes has slowly faded, and gotten replaced by a healthy rosiness from the pink wine, and the wrinkles are still miraculously vanished. I'm going to meet them and dazzle Dwayne with my young looks and confident appearance. He is really going to regret that he let this babe go!

I walk down the closed off streets amongst thousands of expectant football-fans, 99,99% of them men. The sunlight reflects in my hair and I feel tall, blonde and beautiful. A little bit disappointed that not one single man throws me a single glance. Surely I must stand out amongst the crowd? How come football gets men so totally unfocused? When I close in on the statue of Peter 'Ossie' Osgood, the King of Stamford Bridge, and also the place of our rendezvous, I see my two lovely boys on each side of their good-looking father. My own king and our two princes! I start smiling and my eyes water.

'Oh baby! You look stunning!! What have I done? I must have been mad?! Please take me back Andrea' Dwayne bursts out and fall down on his knees.

Eh. no. He doesn't. And I remember that he isn't my own king any more. But at least I refrain to fall on my knees too.

"Quick, we need to get a move on. Is Jason coming back with us later or not?"

Disappointed that Dwayne is being totally unmoved by my new striking looks, I turn to Jason.

"Do you want to stay with me in the FOUR STAR hotel room or come back with your dad later to THAT SMOKEY HOUSE of your grandparents?" I ask my oldest son in Swedish so that he can answer honestly what he wants.

"It depends. Is it going to get boring with you?"

Boring?! BORING?! When is it EVER boring with me?!

"I mean, it is fun being with daddy, and I haven't been with him for so long."

I bet it is fun. Running around in the shops, getting everything you point at, him taking you to places you've never been. But I manage to pretend that I don't only feel dumped and ditched by my ex but also my oldest son, and answer 'sure, you shall stay with him, we'll meet up with them afterwards'. Then I take him to a ridiculously expensive and trendy restaurant for dinner, and afterwards we are watching the game in an overpacked pub, celebrating loudly as Alexander's favorite player Hazard makes the only goal in the game. Boring? Me? Hah!

TWENTY-SEVEN

'Boys have met Gemma'

In the morning I go out for breakfast again. I end up at Le Pain Quotidian in South Kensington and order a banana honey porridge, a Gruyère-cheese croissant and a boule of latte. Again I am in heaven. I am really easily pleased. When I'm finished I call Dwayne but he doesn't answer. They were supposed to go shopping again. I want to tell them not to go mad in the shops. I know Dwayne wants to make up for being a distant father - and now for being a prick against their mother - but I think that drowning them in gifts is not the answer. I text Jason and ask him to tell his dad to call me. Dwayne might not always read texts but I know my son is. Now I don't get any text back though. Maybe they don't want to be interrupted in their shopping spree.

It is a beautiful day and I walk up to Kensington gardens that is showing itself in its best suit. The trees are blossoming in white and pink, which looks lovely against the clear blue sky. Then I cross the road and start to stroll in Hyde Park, but I feel depressed after a while. There is something about walking around alone in there that gets me really moody. I love to walk alone but Hyde Park definitely doesn't do it for me. After another hour with no response from neither my boys nor Dwayne, I walk back to the hotel and call Dwayne again. Still no answer. It feels very familiar and I'm getting seriously pissed off. He has avoided my calls for far too many times for me to react normally to it. I call Jason, who doesn't answer either and that is very unusual. It must be something going on. Suddenly Dwayne calls.

"Hi, everything is alright!"

"I just called to say that you shouldn't buy them everything that they want. You're not Santa Claus you know."

"No, it is alright. I'm happy to give them things since I haven't seen them for so long."

"Don't forget that what you give them has nothing to do with the maintenance that you have to give to me. All this is extra."

"Yeah, I know that."

"Have you spoken to Kate about the boys?"

"No, obviously I want to run it by Sebastian first. You know, she can give him a hard time for knowing about it all along and not having told her."

So - it was really like that then. Sebastian's mother doesn't know that her son has another two half brothers. Poor Sebastian. Having to keep this a secret.

"Listen Dwayne. I don't want anyone to have to keep the boys existence a secret anymore."

"No, I know. I understand that. But Sebastian's mum is crazy and she could really put him through hell."

"Well, according to you all women are crazy."

"But they are."

God, he really doesn't deserve one by his side.

"I guess Jason has told you that they have met Gemma?"

The information hits me hard. It feels like I'm going to faint. What a bastard. I asked him not to introduce her on this trip. Luckily I know him well and I thanked myself for having prepared the boys.

"No" I say weakly, "he hasn't. How did that happen?"

The shock and pain feels like someone ripping off a plaster. My eyes prickle up and I want to crawl into a den.

"Oh it wasn't a big deal. They were fine about it. I asked Jason if he wanted to meet her and he said yes."

"Did you ask Alexander what he wanted?"

"Yeah. He said yes as well, kind of. You know - he wasn't that talkative, but he was fine when he met her."

"How did they meet?" Somehow it feels important to me.

"I went by her house with them, picked her up in the car and dropped her off, so it was very quick. They were fine about it. And they said I have to give them a thousand pounds for them to see her, which is fair enough" he says and laughs. And then he adds "Thank you Andrea. Thank you."

Waking up

Later that afternoon I feel really lonely and miserable. I don't understand where it comes from. One minute I feel on top of the world, self-confident and with new possibilities ahead of me. And the next I feel like the loneliest woman on the planet. Maybe it's the alcohol going in and out of my body. Or just me tumbling against the walls of the confusion room. I force myself to go out for dinner, and return to the place where Jason and I went the day before, Sophie's. The name alone makes me feel safe. I order myself a Sunday roast. Leg of lamb with Shepard's pie, oven roasted parsnips and mint sauce. And a Guinness. And a Bloody Mary. I can't make up my mind and I think I deserve all that I fancy. The Bloody Mary is fantastically spicy and the exact mixture of tomato and saltiness. But it is going straight to my head.

I suddenly realize that the things Dwayne said to me is the same things he had probably said to Gemma. 'Lovely lady' is less threatening to another woman, and he probably called me that. I should be grateful that I'm not 'a crazy bitch' like Sebastian's mother, but somehow I don't feel that. And to say that he was worried that I wouldn't let him see his kids - that is total bullocks. Over the years I have always said to him that I would never keep him from the boys, no matter how angry I was, or if we weren't together. The only one who has kept him from seeing his boys has been himself. Probably it has been a grateful explanation for him to use on Gemma to why he has acted like he has. What a complete asshole. He continues to fabric his truths as they come along. He had a thing for Gemma, but when he was with me he had a thing for me also. Like a donkey stuck between two piles of hay. No doubt he had used our arguments and fall-outs to continue with Gemma without bad conscience, and when he and Gemma had argued he got very loving and affectionate towards me. And took his chance to come over to Stockholm. The last time he came to Stockholm he was a bit distant the first day, but then he started with the cuddling and kissing, and the 'I love you'-s, and it was the same when we were in London. He was always so sad when we left, kept calling me as soon as we got through security, and telling me how much he missed us, sounding all sad and weepy. He had fallen for me, and then some years later, he had fallen for Gemma. And then he had been struggling with which one of us to choose, but of course he chose the easiest way - being with Gemma. Being with me would have involved a move to Stockholm. The funny thing is that I wasn't particularly keen on him moving to Sweden. I was happy continuing the long-distance. But for Dwayne choosing me would mean leaving London. Otherwise Gemma would always be there, lurking. When his foul-play got exploited I had started to doubt what he and I had together, but now I know we were for real. The only problem - BIG problem - was that the third year into our relationship, Gemma had made her entrance, and my relationship with Dwayne started to spiral down. But it still had its glorious moments. As Sophie always says: 'I've seen you together. There is no doubt that you two are a perfect match. You are glowing in each others presence.'

What if Gemma wouldn't have kept him? Would I have started to have doubts, and want him back? Would I be under the impression that I had called it off, and if I wanted to I could take him back? And continue to have a long-distance relationship with him. He would probably meet someone else. Or get back with Gemma again, behind my back. I shiver at the thought. I would never be able to trust him. And what a waste of me - even if passed my expiry-date. Maybe I should be grateful to Gemma. I might not have been able to get out of his infatuating embrace. Maybe I would have continued to live in a lie.

Later on my father calls me.

"Hi! I've sent you an email, maybe you haven't seen it. You must contact us every day. How are you?"

"Well, the boys have met Gemma so I don't feel that great actually."

"Okay. I understand. Tough. What are you doing now?"

"Right now I'm at the hotel and I've had a bath."

"Well stay there. Don't go out."

Feels a bit strange that he all of a sudden has taken on a protective role against his since long grown-up daughter.

"Well I am probably staying in bed, but if I want to go out I will go out."

I'm happy that he is concerned but I am soon-to-be 48. And still my reaction is like the one of a teenager...

"No don't do that, there are so many strange things that can happen. Stay in the room. You'll be home soon."

On the Monday, the third day, I feel really miserable. I feel extremely lonely and I can't wait to get home with my boys. I order Whisky-porridge in the room for breakfast as I can't decide what to do this last day. I really enjoy London, but now I had enough of the alone-time and I'd like to share it with someone. But it is a beautiful day so I finally get out and walk up Exhibition Road to Kensington Garden and Hyde Park again. It is absolutely beautiful with the pink- and white flowering trees. It doesn't perk me up though. Neither does the cappuccino at the Lido Café down by the Serpentine water. I sit in the sun but the wind is chilly, making me shiver.

I get back to South Kensington station and am convinced that I need to eat my way out of the misery I'm feeling. I buy some take-away at Chopstix noodles and sit among other lunch-eating Londoners, at the base of a little statue. I almost get my feet run over by a delivery lorry that is backing up the pedestrian street, which gives me an instant feeling of being invisible again. Until the old man in the lorry worriedly rushes out with a 'sorry love, you'alright?' reminding me of Dwayne's old friend Tom. Which makes me feel visible again, but depressed that the years have flown by.

I walk back to Ca'puccino's, and sit outdoors watching the busy Kings Road. Have to take a detour to not bump into golden boy again, who is still handing out the golden test samples. I have a glass of rosé and a Limonetto this time. I can't have any more food and decide to drink my way through the rest of this trip. After yet another hour, and some shoe-shopping, I pop in to a pub on the way back to the hotel. I feel very calm and content again since I had found TWO pairs of shoes that fits me perfectly. I seat myself indoors but get a table by the open windows, and I have a lovely pint of Guinness in the sun. You can actually eat and drink your way through a whole day.

The pub is slowly filling with Londoners (mostly men) and it is getting more and more chatty in there. I decide to follow my Guinness with a pint of Chelsea Blonde. There you go - I am a Chelsea Blonde! Not that I am that blonde anymore. My hair has darkened after the pregnancies. As well as gone a bit curly in the back, after being completely straight in my younger years. When I wasn't a LADY. I get some curious looks from a couple of the whole male groups, but I probably look all odd when I'm sitting there all on my own.

All of a sudden HE appears. A tall well-dressed grey-haired man with the most beautiful face, and a seven-day beard. Dark-brown eyes and more than a little resemblance to Richard Gere. Is he for real? I try to see if he has got a ring on his finger. Oh hell - does it really matter? I decide to go for it! With the wine and the beer in my spine I feel confident enough to make a move. But before I get a chance to start talking to the hunk, I see how he eyes up a woman passing on the street. When he leans forward and comment her to his friend, who starts to laugh, I say to myself: 'No way'. I have had enough of good looking, too confident men, and decide to stay put on my chair with my blonde beer.

When I'm back at the hotel I slide under the covers with my hand round a steady chunk of a chocolate bar instead of a man. Instant satisfaction without the hassle.

Goodbye. GOOD bye.

I meet up with Dwayne and our beautiful boys the last morning. He is taking us to Gatwick. Jason is sitting in the front passenger seat when I get there, but I do such a very significant jerk with my head and mouth 'back' very clearly, so he has no choice but to crawl into the backseat with Alexander. Dwayne throws a glance at me but very wisely says nothing. As we are driving out of Putney, on the still early morning sleepy streets, I turn to the boys and ask if they've had a good time. The three of them, including Dwayne, starts babbling about what a good time they've had, and what they have been up to. Meeting Dwayne's friend and business partner Jimmy (totally crazy and hilarious), Sebastian (was very quiet), Seb's girlfriend Amanda (was not at all what they expected. They had thought of her as a full-blown all-over pierced Emo, but was nothing of the kind. She was cute). And they had spent some time with granny and grandpa. I am so happy for them, bubbling of happiness over their weekend. Eventually Dwayne turns to me, and innocently asks:

"And how was your weekend?"

It is like pressing a button. Instant anger and hurt wells up inside of me. I don't know where it comes from. A second ago I was sitting being all happy for the boys, but now I feel like I have a hidden lava stream inside of me, that without warning just suddenly breaks through the ground.

"Well it wasn't that good" I say as tears starts to prickle in my eyes. Dwayne has his eyes on the road so he doesn't see the warning signals. The boys hear the tension in my voice though, and I can almost hear their ears growing and shooting out from their heads, to catch every transmitted word.

"Really? Why not?"

"I felt lonely. It was a bit too much time I got to think about things."

"But I thought you liked wandering around on your own?"

"I do. But it was a bit too long, and I told you - I didn't want you to introduce Gemma to the boys this weekend."

"But I asked them and they were fine about it" he says a bit impatiently.

"Well, I wasn't" I burst out with a raised voice. "Right now it feels like I had to pay for half the hotel for you to finally see YOUR boys and you introducing your GIRLFRIEND. And the only thing I got was a 15 minute conversation in the car while you were extremely impatient to get the hell out of there!"

Now he gets angry.

"It is a hell of a time to bring that up now. Aw, look at the boys - you've upset them, they've had such a nice time. Don't destroy it. Why bring this up now? You could have called me at anytime instead of doing this now. You should never talk about things like this in front of the children!"

"I know that Dwayne, but you leave me no choice" I answer angrily after checking the boys and see that they don't look upset at all, only interested. "If you'd know I wanted to talk to you about this you wouldn't answer, let alone come to see me and talk. You always run a mile as soon as it doesn't suit you."

Dwayne's face is all dark as he is holding back his irritation. I decide that it is not the time to push this conversation any further. It is no point. And he is right about one thing - it is not fair on the boys to end their trip with loads of angry screaming. I let us both calm down, and we all sit in silence while we enter the M25. Finally I start to talk again, with a calm voice, to let the boys know that we have passed the minefield.

"This whole thing Dwayne, is a crazy story."

"I know."

"I might write a book about it" I say to test his reactions.

"You can partner up with Gemma then, she seems to be doing loads of writing as well" he answers and laughs.

"Maybe it could be a movie?"

"Yeah, it should be actually."

"Who would play me then?" he asks, always eager for a chance to get a compliment.

"Bradley Cooper" I say and he laughs and nods approvingly. But then I realize my mistake - I have got my favorite actors mixed up.

"No! I mean, what's-his-name, yeah - Gerard Butler!"

One of my other favorite male actors when it comes to something to rest my eyes on. And maybe because he reminds me of Dwayne. Same boyish - but still grown-up - look. Jokey and charming.

"Oh" Dwayne replies, and by his a bit disappointed look I take it that he doesn't know who I mean. Gerard Butler is gorgeous, he should be happy about that.

"Who would play you then?" he asks.

Shit. I should have thought about this. Somehow it feels extremely important which actress should play me in the movie that is never gonna hit the cinemas. How odd. Suddenly one actress pops into my head. Blonde, small tits but big smile, confident and with sparkling eyes, always ready with a joke.

"Yeah, I know! Her - you know, oh - what is her name? Shit. The blonde one. Goldie Hawn's daughter?"

"Oh yeah, I know" he answers with no umphf in his voice.

Bollocks. I should have chosen a more sultry movie-star, like Scarlet Johansson. Or Sienna Miller. But she seems to lack humor. In my youth someone said I looked like Sharon Stone (or maybe I thought so myself?). Someone actually did say I looked like Meryl Streep but that was 30 years ago. Instead I said...well, what's her name? Kate Hudson - that's it. She is not even on the '100 hottest blonde actresses'-list. I should have said Charlize Theron. She's number eight at least.

"Who would play Gemma then?" I ask bravely. I need to know.

"Um…. let me think… I know! What's her name? Eh… the one in Armageddon. The singers daughter."

You have got to be kidding me.

"Liv Tyler?"

"Yes! That's it! She would play Gemma!"

"Oh, Dwayne, for fuck's sake!"

"What?" he says innocently.

"Liv Tyler? Come ON! Why don't you just stab me in the heart with a knife!" I moan and hit my fist hard on my chest, where my heart once was.

"Yeah? Why?"

"Tall, big breast and pouty lips for instance!"

Dwayne laughs and the boys giggle in the backseat.

"And long, brown hair and come-and-get-me eyes."

"Yup. That's it!"

"I KNEW IT! Jeez… I'm never gonna recover from this" I mutter.

I'm sorry Kate Hudson but you can never compete with Liv Tyler when it comes to keeping a man attached to you.

Somehow it feels nice to talk so easily about this. And it is a very well-known jokey atmosphere between us. Maybe we can keep this spirit up between us. Despite what's happened. Everything is so easy with Dwayne. As long as it's not something serious.

When we arrive at the airport I hand him a written

agreement. Even though we can joke and laugh I think it is better to be safe than sorry.

"Here is a suggestion for an economic agreement between us Dwayne."

"Yeah? What does it say?"

"Just look it through and let me know what you think. For example: it says that you shall make sure that you see the boys at least three times a year."

"Oh, we're going to meet a lot more than that from now on!"

Really, I'm thinking. We'll see about that.

When we get out of the car all of us hug, and Dwayne and I kiss each other on the mouth, like we've always done. Feels so familiar and comforting. Maybe we can have a friendly, sensible relationship from now on? Act mature and grown-up.

On the plane I discover from the boys chatting, that what I had thought was a quick intro to Gemma actually was a 5-hour session. Including a couple of hours in her home where Jason played the guitar for her, and a chicken dinner at a restaurant in town. She wore sneakers, had a fit body (of course...) and had about the same color of hair as me but a bit reddish (aaaaargh! I always wanted red hair!). And she had been a model. OF COURSE!! A f-cking model.

They also tell me that they saw a photo with Dwayne and Gemma, where she was pregnant.

"Pregnant?" I say to Jason who reveals this. "Pregnant? But she couldn't have been when she and your dad met? She had her child years before she started dating him? With another man. Are you sure she was pregnant?"

"She wasn't pregnant, she was just fat" says Alexander.

Now why would a woman - any woman - have a photo on display where she looks fat?

"Daddy was fat in the picture too" Alexander continues.

Jason looks puzzled.

Jesus, of course Dwayne lied about that too.

"Are you sure that it was Gemma and daddy in the photo? Maybe it was someone else? Like her parents? Or her daughter? Did they look the same age?"

The boys don't seem to want to continue the subject though and replies with a 'oh, I don't know' and that is the end of it. I don't want to pursue. It is not fair on them. Fuck, I'm thinking. Gemma wrote that they had been through good and bad things. Was this one of them? Being pregnant and losing it? Does it matter to me? Yes! By the way I am reacting, feeling nauseous, it IS important to me. But more the fact that he is continuing the lying. Why can't he just be open about things? Does he really believe that it is better to not know? And when the hell was he expecting a baby with her?! If he was. I can't be sure of course, but it can explain why he got so angry all of a sudden during our closure talk. Hit a sore spot. And it would definitely explain why he couldn't make a choice in the past, digging himself deeper and deeper in quicksand.

TWENTY-EIGHT

Armageddon

Back home I think that it was a good thing to have some kind of a closure talk after all. Even if short. It is a process you have to go through, you can't skip some of the steps. I feel alright. Thinking we can have a friendly relationship. Not just me and Dwayne, but also me and Gemma. She and I probably have loads to talk about. What happened has happened. There is no way to change that.

I start to think about the past. If Dwayne wasn't able to handle a long-distance relationship - why the hell did he perk me up talking about 'presence strengthens - absence sharpens'? It had made me feel we were on the same page regarding us being together but living apart. When it really was more like 'Out of sight - out of mind'. When he was with me Gemma didn't exist. He was with us, and was the boys father and my boyfriend full stop. And when he came back to Gemma he was with her. And we were out of his mind. Or at least I was out of his mind. The boys were probably there. But he couldn't talk about them of course, since 'he didn't see them very much'. Especially not Alexander. Who actually didn't exist in the Gemma-world.

One early morning, before work and school starts, I hear Jason singing in the bathroom. No doubt while fixing his hair in front of the mirror. The time in the bathroom exceeds with two minutes a day, and he will soon have to get up in the middle of the night to make it in time to school. This morning I discover that he has a new song to his repertoire. Aerosmith's 'I don't want to miss a thing'. A very powerful ballad sung by the ever so rough looking Steven Tyler. The song brings back memories of Dwayne calling me from time to time, often from his car, and excitedly saying 'Listen baby'! Then turning the volume up, making my eyes water hearing the fantastic lyrics. Especially when played by the one you're in love with.

'I could stay awake just to hear you breathing
Watch you smile when you are sleeping
While you're far away and dreaming
I could spend my life in this sweet surrender
I could stay lost in this moment forever
Every moment spent with you is a moment I treasure'

The single was released in August 1998, about the time when Dwayne and I really got together, and Dwayne has played it to me over the years. The last time actually not that long before his double-life came up to the surface. Now why would I suspect that he was into someone else while playing THIS song to me?

'Lying close to you feeling your heart beating
And I'm wondering what you're dreaming,
Wondering if it's me you're seeing
Then I kiss your eyes and thank God we're together
And I just wanna stay with you
In this moment forever, forever and ever'

Oh, he REALLY misses me!! As much as I am missing him!

'Don't wanna close my eyes
I don't wanna fall asleep
'Cause I'd miss you, baby
And I don't wanna miss a thing

'Cause even when I dream of you
The sweetest dream would never do
I'd still miss you, baby
And I don't wanna miss a thing'

Well you're missing hell of a lot I could think if I was irritated or angry with him for one or the other reason when he called. Usually for not making arrangements to come over. I would remind him that he was missing out on most parts of his boys' childhood. But mostly it got me feeling very close to him, although apart.

When I go to work I can't stop thinking about the song. There is something nagging in the back of my head trying to get my attention. Hang on. It can't be...? I google the song and there it is. It is the lead movie soundtrack of Armageddon. Starring Liv Tyler... I start to laugh. Fuck. Has he played that song to her as well? If she moaned about them not living together? Or when he suddenly had to leave for, let's say, 'a business trip', or needed to spend some time with his parents or Sebastian? Now I really doubt that he has played it exclusively to me. My mind starts spinning. It feels like everything has come full circle, but I can't see where the circle starts and finishes. Did he play the song to me and thought of Gemma aka Liv Tyler? Or did he feel that we were the same person, only that one was situated in Sweden and one materialized in London? 'Every moment spent with you BOTH is a moment I treasure'... Talk about getting two things in one. We were probably like a Kinder egg to him.

The movie Armageddon premiered in July 1998, when I met Dwayne for the first time. The story of my life with him suddenly feels similar to the plot in the film. A giant catastrophe waiting to happen. I just can't figure out if the asteroid threatening to destroy the Earth is Dwayne or Gemma. I decide that the asteroid is Gemma. Always been out there in space. Her first email suddenly got her to visualize for the first time on the radar (or whatever instrument they use to keep track of big dangerous objects swirling around out there). In Gemma's perspective it is probably me though. Then I change my mind. The asteroid is Dwayne. Destroying both Gemma's world and mine as we knew it. Unlike in the movie with its happy ending. Fuck. Why didn't someone blow it in pieces before it smashed? It did almost implode itself when Dwayne had his heart-failure back in 2003/2004. I wish it had. Then I could have kept all our memories in fluffy pink clouds. Then I regret that immediately. The boys are better off with a dad that they know and who is alive - even if he is a dickhead - instead of a dead one that they hardly would have any memories of. Actually Gemma did drill some holes into the Dwayne-asteroid when she started asking him about if he thought he had any more kids. And when she got the shocking info about a second child with me, and saw my photos on Facebook, she decided to throw in some nuclear weapons into the holes in the format of emails which detonated when opened. When exploding, big parts of the asteroid hit both her and me hard on the head and in the heart, but rocks fell down on Ellen and Paul as well. And little stones fell, and will keep falling, on Dwayne's three sons.

'I just wanna hold you close
I feel your heart so close to mine
And just stay here in this moment
For all the rest of time'

No doubt Dwayne is a man who is convinced that wherever he lays his hat at the moment is his current home.

A strong woman moves on - a woman scorned wants revenge...

Although I feel content and ready to move on there is something still nagging me. Probably caused by the too short closure talk with Dwayne, not being able to play along and do it properly. It drives me mad that all this seems to just have caused a minor bump in Dwayne's path of life.

· Gemma is still with him.
· He still has his job.
· His sons are forgiving.
· His parents are still by his side.
· His friends probably admire him a bit. Juggling two great women at the same time. One ex-model and one... well... swede.

I want this to cause - if not a roller-coaster-ride - then at least a very rocky road for him for at least 12, no 16, years onwards. He has been a bastard in the past, now I can be a bitch in the future! I want him to suffer at least a bit. Not because he is human. After all, people fall in love even if they are engaged in someone else. That happens. And I do understand that Dwayne didn't tell me he was married when we first met. If he had done that then Jason wouldn't exist. I realize that he didn't tell Gemma that he was expecting another child with a woman in Sweden when he started to fancy her. If she left her partner within a week after shagging Dwayne I can understand that he didn't tell Gemma about me. If she did such a life-changing thing because of him it would have demanded a lot of courage on his behalf to spill the beans. And when he came to me in Sweden, holding his newborn Alexander for the first time, and his soon to be three years old Jason cuddling and kissing him. Of course he didn't say 'oh, by the way, I have humped someone else, what do you think we should do?'. As the years go by I do understand that it gets harder and harder to tell the truth. Especially if he has feelings for both. I can comprehend all this.

But still.

No, I want to punish him for the way he has handled this. First by letting it go on for too long, and then for neglecting to handle it when it finally came out. Most of all for being such a coward and not man-up about it, and on HIS OWN initiative face up to me. What does Dwayne dislike? To let people know his business. Nosiness. Whiny and nagging women. Talk about things, like emotions and digging in the past. I review my revenge options.

1. Kill him. Funny that the first thing that came to mind was that. But again - no. I don't want him to die. And it would be SO TYPICAL Dwayne to disappear from the troubles he has caused. No, I want him to develop a conscience and live for a veeeeery long time, and suffer in the meantime. Or maybe it would be possible to bury him à la Stephen King in a 'sematary' from where he can crawl up as a changed man. A nice and honest man? Eh, no. That is not possible.

2. Withhold him from seeing his sons. No point. He manages very well to withhold himself from seeing his sons. He doesn't need me for that. And I want the boys to be with their father and absorb some of his good qualities, like... like... Well there must be some, I just can't remember them right now.

3. Write a book about this so my version gets known among his friends and acquaintances.

It is when I read my revenge option number three that I start to think that I might be on to something. Maybe I CAN make time for it? And there are loads of self-publishing companies nowadays, aren't there? It will be like catching two flies in one go. People will know his business. Instead of going to a therapist I can write everything down and process it along the way. And when it is finished I can give a signed copy to Gemma and Kate. And maybe his second wife if I can find her. The one everyone probably thinks Dwayne left because of me. When it really was because of Gemma. She has actually wrecked two relationships (at least). His second marriage and my relationship with Dwayne. Maybe she was involved in the crash of his first marriage as well?

Anyway, I could continue to write down my thoughts, and what happens. And I have got the emails and texts.

He won't escape from this. I WILL tell my story. Both how we met, and how our relationship imploded. From my perspective, how I experienced it. And I will tell the world. Let everyone around him hear about his foul play.
Advice to you adulterers out there - never leave the conversation until BOTH have had enough...

To all my fellow deceived sisters and brothers:
If you see a good-looking hunk of a man walking the streets of London - with a Marlon Brando body (nowadays not so young), lush Paul Newman lips, and a broad Gene Kelly smile - then say hello from Andrea. A Hunter too good to be true!

The End.

Or...?

EPILOGUE

Didn't I ever suspect anything?

You must think I'm crazy, or a fool.
How come I never guessed?
After all - he did have awfully loads of time on his own.
Didn't I wonder what he was doing over there in swinging London? I must have seen it coming.
But. I managed to stay true, why wouldn't he?

You should be convinced that your partner is faithful to you, fidelity is the base of every relationship. But let's face it - we are not more than humans. In a relationship there is always a possibility that your partner is cheating. Although a long-distance relationship has enough challenges. I didn't need the extra burden of doubt as well. And since everyone we met in London acted like everything was normal - his friends, his brother and family, the other relatives, his business partner (whom I never met but talked to over the phone), his son and above all his parents - how could I have known?

But of course there were things in the past that got me wondering.

Suspicion number 1 - the disappearing acts:

Just shut his phone off for days. I hated it. What if something happened to the boys and I needed to get hold of him? It just happened 3 or 4 times during our relationship, but still. The first times I pondered until I got crazy - was it something I had said, was he angry? upset? sad? He could never explain it afterwards. He blamed his mother and said that he probably was mentally disturbed due to the fact that she had thrown him out when he was 16. Poor thing. But no - that he was on holiday with someone else never crossed my mind.

Suspicion number 2 - sudden jealousy:

When Jason was small, and Alexander a year or less, Dwayne suddenly got very jealous. He kept accusing me of eyeing other men up, and I got really irritated about it. He had never shown any tendencies before but now he did. I thought it was due to hormones produced by a protective father but now I understand. 'It takes one to know one'.

Suspicion number 3 - winning the lottery:

Once when I was really angry with Dwayne, maybe (probably) because he vanished out of radar again, I bought myself a lottery ticket. It was in the early fall of 2003, when Alexander just had started nursery. I thought that if I'm not lucky in love I might be lucky in gambling. I bought the lottery ticket, scraped it and won £10.000 on the spot. 'What the hell has he done?!?' was my first thought. Now I know. He had shagged Gemma.

I bought my little cottage for the money, so it was worth something to be unlucky in love.

Suspicion number 4 - the wedding-nonvitation:

When it was time for Dwayne's brother to marry his Catherine 10 years ago, I didn't get an invitation. Neither from them or Dwayne himself asking me. I didn't know if I should take that as an 'OF COURSE you are invited - you don't need an invitation'. After a l l was the mother of two sons of the spouse's brother. The boys were 6 and 3 at the time and since I didn't get any guidance from Dwayne if I should bring the boys or not, I eventually decided not to go. I was pretty tired anyway with two young boys and working full-time, and Dwayne himself said that he wasn't that keen on going - 'hate weddings, they're going to divorce anyway' he informed me. But in the end he went. Afterwards, when I asked him about it, he said that it had been surprisingly fun.

I wonder if he took Gemma there. Or someone else...?

Suspicion number 5 - the family tree, lacking three:

When we finally were invited to a family gathering, at the birthday of Dwayne's grandmother with his father's cousins and their children, I got shown a picture of a family tree that she had gotten at her ninetieth birthday the year before. My heart sank when I saw 'Dwayne & Kate' in one of the squares and then a little arrow pointing at square 'Sebastian'. Jason and Alexander were tumbling around in the garden - a very vivid evidence of their existence - but on the family tree they just weren't. I tried to explain to myself that the fact that I wasn't in the picture must be because we weren't married, but why ALL Dwayne's sons wasn't there made me feel sick. Did they consider them bastards? Was this family really that old fashioned? I didn't dare to say anything at the party but when we came back to Ellen & Paul's house in the evening I confessed to Dwayne's mother how it had made me feel. 'Oh, I wouldn't let it get stuck in my head, they probably had it made years ago', and Dwayne just dismissed me with a 'don't be silly'.
I didn't let it get stuck in my head, but for sure it was like a sticker pasted on my heart.

Suspicion number 6 - the unsupportive friend:

When Dwayne came over here in 2007, with a bag (about the size of a teabag) with his few belongings, for 'ready to settle down in Sweden'-attempt number one (or ready - he got nauseous from day one over his decision), he told me what his best friend at the time had said to him when he left. 'You must be mad. You will never feel at home in

Stockholm. You love London.' I was pretty pissed off at that so called friend. How could he be so unsupportive when Dwayne was on his way to move to his young boys? Even the cab-driver taking him to the airport had been more supportive with his 'good luck over there'. No wonder Dwayne got cold feet straight away. Probably the friend had actually said: 'You must be mad. You will never feel at home there. You love Gemma.' That makes his friend's words a little bit more understandable.

Suspicion number 7 - 'sometimes we don't see him for days':

Some years ago Dwayne's mother said in a by-the-way manner, while we were sitting in their kitchen, that 'sometimes we don't see Dwayne for days'. Since he was living there it was kind of odd, and I wonder if she tried to tell me something. But just weeks before, Dwayne had started talking about how many night-gigs he had on his new working site, and that there were loads of emergency calls about leaking pipes that he had to deal with (well I bet!).

In hindsight I should have understood of course, and followed it up with a question. Why didn't I? Didn't I want to hear the answer? But I know that if I would have asked his mother about it she wouldn't have told me. Or said 'what you don't know won't hurt you'. But then I would have known. I wouldn't have let that one pass, like Gemma did. I think.

Suspicion number 8 - the pat on the shoulder:

We hadn't seen each other for months, it might have been somewhere in 2011-12, and as we went into his bed we kissed goodnight and then he patted me on the shoulder, turned his back to me, and fell asleep. I really should have known then.

Suspicion number 9 - the sleep-over at the brothers family:

The pat on the shoulder made me think that we needed some time to ourselves, to look into each others eyes again and be man and woman, not just mum and dad. We were invited to dinner at Dwayne's brother and his family and when I was alone in the kitchen with his wife Catherine, I asked her if the boys could stay with them and their two boys for the night and I could take Dwayne for a drink. I told her I was desperate for some alone-time with him. 'Sorry, that's not possible. I could need some alone-time with my hubby myself.' I was taken aback, her usually so easygoing attitude, like nothing is a problem, was replaced by a depreciative look and I felt ashamed for asking. She probably was working hard and wanted to relax in the evening when we would leave, and didn't want to take care of another two boys, even if they had a great time playing together. So I was a bit surprised when she after dinner asked if we all wanted to spend the night at their house. When I think about it now I think it must be that Catherine actually wasn't that comfortable helping Dwayne juggling his two girlfriends.

Suspicion number 10 - the local pub:
Close to Dwayne and his parent's house there's a pub
called The Spencer that has been renovated to attract the
30-40-something who needs a bit more trendy style, but it
had still managed to keep its genuine atmosphere. I
thought it was super to have such a place on walking
distance, especially when they in the summertime also has
outdoor seating in the adjacent park at the Putney
common. But Dwayne refused to take me there. He said he
knew the owners and didn't like them, and claimed that he
had been kicked out from that bar after being involved in a
fight once. He always had to drive us to pubs further away
when my cravings for a pint of Guinness became too
strong.
Maybe he did know the owners. And they knew both him
and Gemma.

Suspicion number 11 - the ring-thing:
In one of the trips to Isle of Wight, Dwayne bought me a
ring with a big, black pearl between two small diamonds. I
fell in love with it as soon as I saw it behind the counter. It
was extraordinary and really stood out amongst the
smaller white and pinkish ones. I was on the verge of
buying it myself, but Dwayne took out his wallet and paid
for it. I wore it every day for years. The pearl reminded me
of my big hunk of a man, and the two small diamonds of
our sons. But one day the big, black pearl was gone. Just
came off its attachment somewhere between work and
home. Talk about signs...

Suspicion number 12 - toiletries vanishing:

His bathroom at his parents got emptier and emptier the last couple of years. Suddenly there were no aftershaves left, and less toiletries. I noted it, but I also knew that he didn't like to have loads of stuff around him. Since I am a collector and have my bathroom overfilled with stuff, I just registered that we were different.

Suspicion number 13 - photos disappearing:

He had his room covered with pictures of the boys and me, and on one visit they were gone, and just one remained - a close-up photo of me and the boys together. But as I said - he didn't like too much stuff around.

Suspicion number 14 - didn't give me his new work email:

'It is set up for work, and several people can read it'.
Okay. Can you say something about that really? You don't want your partner's colleagues reading emails from you. (Especially not if they are your partner's lover...).

Suspicion number 15 - the Facebook-outburst:

Late in June 2014, a little more than a month before Gemma's first email arrived, Dwayne called me and was angry. Which was strange. He never called me when angry - he just disappeared.
"I don't want you to publish photos of me on Facebook. I don't like it!"
"What are you on about? I have only published a couple of photos of you over the years. And you seemed happy then.

I told you about it and you got loads of likes and friends saying that you were good looking - and you laughed."

"Well I don't want you to do it now" he said with a humpf. "Are you still a friend of Catherine on Facebook? I don't want my brother to know my whereabouts."

Dwayne had fallen out with his brother a couple of years ago, and according to Dwayne he had tried to sort it out, but his brother and his wife didn't want anything to do with him any more. I am pretty sure that it takes two to tango, and that Dwayne wasn't as grown-up in this as he pretended.

"Hey, who I am friends with on Facebook is none of your business. And don't drag me into your conflicts. I like your brother and his wife."

"Just don't put pictures of me in there!"

"Okay, I won't!" I said and two hours later I texted him:

Just published an album on Facebook with 20 photos of you!

But honestly - that didn't get me suspicious. I only thought he was paranoid.

Suspicion number 16 - very long text from him after a quarrel:
Now THAT was almost the most suspicious thing of all! It actually made me think that he was in a relationship with another woman. He had never expressed himself in that way before. Suddenly very understanding about my

feelings and how his behavior during the quarrel had affected me. But since it seemed to have gotten him emotionally and mentally developed I kind of enjoyed it. Didn't think it could be more than a brief affair though... that had ended.

Hmm... Seems like there were plenty of things to be suspicious about after all. But it's not until you put them all together that the pattern gets clear. To every suspicious behavior there will always be an answer. Either from your partner or from yourself. Feeling suspicious is tormenting, and the explanations makes you feel that you're a fool, or a hysterical bitch. You don't want to be that. You want to be strong and confident.
My strategy has always been: trust - until proven untrustworthy. And look where it got me.
My advice to you? Put your different suspicions on post-its and lay the puzzle...

ACKNOWLEDGEMENTS

My beautiful **J & A**, thank you for existing, and thank you for putting up with your crazy mum while she's been writing this book. For being supportive while she had to get this story about your dad out of her head. I love you.

And THANK YOU **S** for being there for me thick-and-thin! My own emergency-ward, on-call 24/7. Thank you for being my memory stick when my own brain has gone blank, and for sharing your most intimate details. You would be the perfect partner for me. I'm so sad we are not lesbians. It would've been so much easier and fun!

Thank you **mum & dad**, for helping me to raise the boys over the years, the uncountable picking-ups at nursery, cooking lunches, dinners, serving snacks, helping me with both house and home - I owe you everything!

Dear **brother**, thank you for being a male role model for the boys, always wanting what's best for them, and for helping me with various things over the years even if I sometimes suffer from the 'big-sister'-syndrome.
And thank you for having a lovely **girlfriend**.

My fantastic, supportive friends **A, M, K**! Thank you for all the things we have experienced together, growing up from cocky teenagers to responsible parents, house owners, managers, partners.

Thank you **A** for the weird stories of real life making me feel I'm not the only one surrounded by crazy exes.

Thank you my dear cousin **M**, for sharing your stories, and for always being on the lookout for a new man for me.

Thank you my friends **C** & **G** and **L**, for embracing me, and for including me in your life. Here's to past and upcoming holidays! And big thanks to my Norwegian armada: **T, K, E, M, T**.

Thank you **work colleagues** for the encouraging pep talks! Even though you didn't have a clue what the book would be about in the beginning, you just gave me warming cheer ups. A special thank you **C** who got me in contact with a REAL author, and **H** who introduced me to my very first test reader **A**! From her I got such valuable input, especially on the first chapter, and alerted me about the out-of-context words that I thought I was using right.

Thank you **P** for joining the Swedish B-cup tour in 1998! And **K** for connecting me with test reader number two, **E**.

To my fellow soon-to-be and newborn **Authors from Tara magazine's writing course:** LOVE! You really got me going!

Thank you dear, dear **readers** of my blog and all of you that has contacted me after hearing about my story in magazines, papers and on telly.

Thank you **E** - I hate you. Or no, I don't. I think. Talk about mixed emotions. In some way you are the reason that my man, the father of my boys, hasn't longed for our company since you have been on a shorter distance. But it is not your fault. I am grateful that you contacted me. Somehow I admire you. If it had to be someone I'm glad it's you. Thank you for arranging trips so the boys get to see their father. I will be there for you to pick up the pieces if you realize that this is not a man you want by your side. I'll even help you write the sequel to this book; 'Gemma's story'. We are eager to hear it!

And last and therefore least: **W**. Thank you for being the man that you are, not being responsible and cautious. If you hadn't been who you are, and if my body hadn't responded to yours in the way that it did, our beautiful boys wouldn't exist. Now they do, and for that I am eternally grateful to you. I could have done without the restless nights trying to understand you, the tears I've spilled, and the doubting in myself thinking I needed to act differently. You have been a prick in the past, now I'll be a bitch in the future. Still: You were always on my mind and I will always love you. To quote Rod Stewart:

'I would not change a thing, if I could do it all over again
What I'm trying to say in this awkward way is
I still love you'

Johnny O'Reilly... Still there? You know where to find me!

Confused?

So was I...

If you want to see the timeline of a two... three-timer
you are welcome to visit my blog:

ahuntertoogoodtobetrue.wordpress.com

or join me on Facebook or Twitter
for photos and progress:

@ahuntertoogoodtobetrue

@AHunter_TGTBT